Dr. … moment he strode into the room, still wearing his scrubs, his hair disheveled from the cap he'd just removed.

Kendra Jenkins got to her feet. "Hello, Dr. Dash," she said, her words husky.

Aaron could only stare at the woman he'd never forgotten. She's even more special than I remembered, he thought, taking her in from head to toe. How well I recall the way those green eyes of hers can glint with suppressed anger, yet seem completely vulnerable the next moment. She has hair like a goddess. And that mouth . . . How did I keep from kissing it on that night so long ago?

The silence between them was thick with tension brought about by their memories.

"So," he said finally, "you're back."

Dear Reader,

October is a very special month at Silhouette Romance. We're celebrating the most precious love of all . . . a child's love. Our editors have selected five heartwarming stories that feature happy-ever-afters with a family touch—*Home for Thanksgiving* by Suzanne Carey, *And Daddy Makes Three* by Anne Peters, *Casey's Flyboy* by Vivian Leiber, *Paper Marriage* by Judith Bowen and *Beloved Stranger* by Peggy Webb.

But that's not all! We're also continuing our WRITTEN IN THE STARS series. This month we're proud to present one of the most romantic heroes in the zodiac—the Libra man—in Patricia Ellis's *Pillow Talk*.

I hope you enjoy this month's stories, and in the months to come, watch for Silhouette Romance novels by your all-time favorites, including Diana Palmer, Brittany Young, Annette Broadrick and many others.

The authors and editors of Silhouette Romance books strive to bring you the best of romance fiction, stories that capture the laughter, the tears—the sheer joy—of falling in love. Let us know if we've succeeded. We'd love to hear from you!

Happy Reading,

Valerie Susan Hayward
Senior Editor

SUZANNE CAREY

Home for Thanksgiving

Silhouette Romance
Published by Silhouette Books New York
America's Publisher of Contemporary Romance

SILHOUETTE BOOKS
300 E. 42nd St., New York, N.Y. 10017

HOME FOR THANKSGIVING

ISBN: 0-373-08825-6

First Silhouette Books printing October 1991

Printed in the U.S.A.

Books by Suzanne Carey

Silhouette Romance

A Most Convenient Marriage #633
Run, Isabella #682
Virgin Territory #736
The Baby Contract #777
Home for Thanksgiving #825

Silhouette Desire

Kiss and Tell #4
Passion's Portrait #69
Mountain Memory #92
Leave Me Never #126
Counterparts #176
Angel in His Arms #206
Confess to Apollo #268
Love Medicine #310
Any Pirate in a Storm #368

Silhouette Intimate Moments

Never Say Goodbye #330
Strangers When We Meet #392

SUZANNE CAREY

is a former reporter and magazine editor who prefers to write romance novels because they add to the sum total of love in the world.

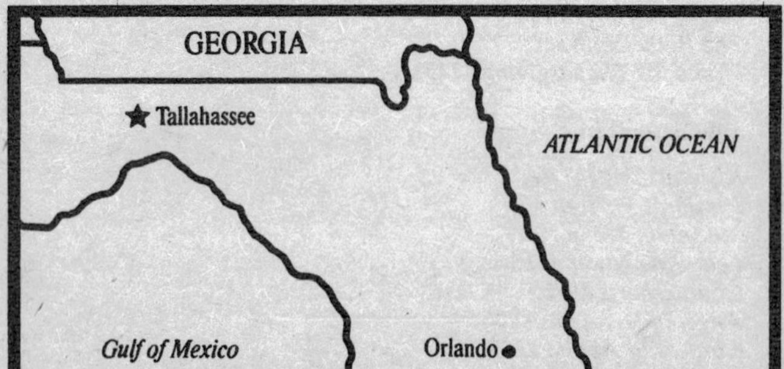
GEORGIA
Tallahassee
ATLANTIC OCEAN
Gulf of Mexico
Orlando
Tampa
St. Petersburg
FLORIDA
N
Miami

Prologue

"Mrs. Jenkins...what's this about the wrong IV solution for the Carradine child?"

The question, put by Dr. Aaron Dash, was flint hard. Kendra blinked as it pierced her fog of unhappy emotions. As head nurse on the Surgical Intensive Care Unit, anything that happened there was her responsibility. "I don't know, doctor," she answered, anxiously scanning the chart.

She was keenly aware of his scowling expression, not to mention the bland, expectant faces of Dr. Hanley Tyler, chief of staff at Children's Memorial, and Bess Martin, the hospital's director of nursing. Despite her effort to remain calm, dealing with an irate physician was almost more than she could handle at the moment.

The quarterly visit of Bess and Dr. Tyler was routine and yet it wasn't. What made it special this time, and more than a little nerve-racking, was that Aaron was present, as well. A tall, dark-haired man with arresting hazel eyes, the new chief cardiologist had quickly acquired a reputation for being a stickler when it came to patient care. She'd heard he was extremely tough over the most minor infraction.

Of course, he'd been recruited from Johns Hopkins in Baltimore for his medical ability, not his genius at public relations. Serious about her work despite the crushing anguish that ruled her personal life, Kendra valued his opinion of her work.

Two notations on the chart quickly caught her eye. The first, consisting of some scribbled initials that might have been hers but weren't, belonged to the new nurse on the unit, Kim Johanssen. Below them was an acknowledgment, also in Kim's handwriting, that an error had been made. Dextrose had been given in one-quarter-strength saline solution instead of distilled water. It was a mistake, thank heaven, that wouldn't have a deleterious effect on the patient.

Determinedly Kendra met her questioner's gaze. "I'm sorry, doctor," she said. "I didn't realize this had happened. You'll note that less than one hundred cc of the saline solution was given before the error was rectified."

Her words struck a spark of indignation. "What do you mean, *didn't realize?*" he snapped. "Aren't those your initials on the chart?"

Kendra was about to defend herself, then hesitated. Kim was still in her preliminary employment period and could be fired for the error. Yet she was an excellent nurse, warm and caring with the unit's young patients. And she definitely needed the job. Kendra decided not to say anything.

Aaron drew his brows more ominously together. "If I were you, Mrs. Jenkins," he warned, "I'd be careful not to let this happen again...particularly not with one of my patients. If the error had involved some other substance, narcotics for instance, I'd have been forced to recommend peer review."

Though Kendra flushed, she didn't frame a retort. Okay, she thought. I asked for it by shielding Kim. But I'll be darned if I'll apologize again.

Giving her a searching look, Aaron flipped to another chart. He found himself wishing he hadn't leaned on her quite so hard. Though he guessed Kendra Jenkins had a temper that matched her abundant auburn hair, she'd faced up to her error like a true professional. She didn't deserve the extra dig. I wonder what's bothering her? he thought, allowing himself a moment's contemplation before returning to the business at hand. Surely the world of pain I sense in those big green eyes didn't spring exclusively from my dressing-down.

Moments later a minor crisis erupted and the unit staff handled it expertly under Kendra's direction. Aaron didn't comment.

"Let's have supper sometime next week," Bess Martin suggested, lingering for a moment after Aaron and Dr. Tyler had gone. "I'd like you to think about taking some time off. With everything that's been going on in your life, you need it. I don't want to lose one of my best people to stress."

Kendra shrugged, attempting to make light of her situation. "I will if you want me to, Bess," she answered. "But honestly, I'm okay. Right now, work is my saving grace."

Hovering nearby, Kim approached Kendra's desk as soon as the director of nursing was out of earshot. "Thanks for not throwing me to the wolves a few minutes ago," she said. "I hope it didn't get you in any trouble."

Dismissing the possibility with a shake of her head, Kendra was forced to exercise iron control over a sudden prickling of tears. Please, she thought. Don't let one more person bark at me. *Or* speak to me with kindness. I'm not sure I can handle it.

"Don't let Dr. Dash's manner upset you," she advised briskly, waving her assistant back to work. "Just be sure to double-check everything from now on. Triple-check if it's one of his patients."

That evening Kendra kept going until well past midnight, staying overtime to help stabilize a young accident victim who had just arrived. Finally she was free to go. Exhausted, she headed for the parking lot.

It was a beautiful night. The heat of the day, so oppressive when she'd arrived for work around 3:00 p.m., had been washed away by late-afternoon thundershowers. Balmy and seductive, a light breeze whispered how sad it was to be alone.

Overcome by a rush of emotion, she sagged against her car, heedless of the dew that dampened her uniform. Believing herself unobserved at last, she gave way to a flood of tears. A month earlier, the body of her husband, an air force surgeon on temporary duty in the Philippines, had been returned to the United States for burial. Major Glenn Jenkins had been killed in an automobile accident near Clark Air Base along with a fellow officer and two enlisted men.

Though she'd sensed for some time their marriage was in trouble, Kendra had been overcome with grief. We were happy in the beginning, she'd tried to tell herself. A few days later even that dubious comfort was stripped away by a letter Glenn had posted a few hours before his death.

Never one to face up to unpleasantness in person, Glenn had waited until he was thousands of miles distant to in-form her that he'd been having an affair. She'd gone numb with shock when she read that his lover, a Chinese-Cambodian woman who worked as a civilian aide at Tampa's Macdill Air Force Base, Glenn's permanent station, was two months pregnant.

Stunned by her husband's death and shaken by his infidelity, she'd found his news about the baby the most difficult thing to bear. Though Glenn hadn't particularly wanted children, she *had*—desperately. Yet to her sorrow, that option had been closed to her as a teen. The fact that he'd found it easy to impregnate someone else had twisted a knife in her heart.

In the letter, Glenn had added insult to injury by telling her not to worry—he'd make sure his lover had an abortion on his return! Hadn't he understood Kendra would *never* have wanted or condoned such a thing, particularly not for her sake?

"I was a fool to get mixed up with Song in the first place," he'd concluded with barely a hint of contrition. "I can only hope you'll forgive me. If we divorced, my career would suffer. And you'd lose your military benefits."

I wonder what would have happened if he'd come back from the Philippines alive? she asked herself as she wept in the hospital parking lot. Probably I'd have left him. Maybe then he'd have stopped talking abortion and married the mother of his child.

"Anything I can do to help?"

The deep male voice at Kendra's elbow made her jump. Oh, no! she thought, rummaging in her purse for a tissue. The last thing I need is for Aaron Dash to see me in this state. "I'm fine," she answered. "Really. I don't need your help."

For a moment Aaron regarded her with uncertainty, wondering if she'd shrug off physical contact. He decided to chance it. Gently, so as not to provoke a defensive reaction, he slipped one arm about her shoulders.

"You haven't convinced me," he said, his tone as friendly and nonthreatening as he could make it. "You have an excellent reputation. For you to screw up an IV tells me something's gone pretty wrong in your life. I trust all those tears don't stem from what happened upstairs?"

Mutely Kendra shook her head. To her chagrin her bottom lip was quivering.

"Thank goodness. Want to go somewhere and talk?"

About to give him a resounding *no,* Kendra reconsidered. For the past several weeks she'd bottled up her grief and rage until she felt as if she must explode. There simply hadn't been anyone she felt comfortable talking with. She didn't have any close family left. And she was much too private to discuss Glenn's treachery with her friends at the hospital or the wives of his fellow officers.

Tonight she'd reached the end of her rope. Without some means of venting her feelings, she doubted if she'd get any sleep. Could she trust Aaron Dash to keep a confidence? What would he say if she broke down and told him of her pain?

Studying her, Aaron guessed how proud she could be—and how close she was to coming apart. "C'mon," he said, his usual concern for the hurt and dispossessed overcoming any hesitance he had about barging into her life. "You can cry at my place."

The will to resist wrung out of her, Kendra wanted to collapse against him. "My car..." she began.

"I'll bring you back to it when you're feeling better. In the meantime it'll be okay here. You're in no condition to drive, anyway...unless you have windshield wipers on those big green eyes."

Kendra's mouth curved despite her tears.

Situated on the second floor of an older, two-story building, Aaron's apartment faced the bay and some city-owned tennis courts across the street. It was modest but oddly stylish, like his Karmann-Ghia convertible. She glanced at a wall of books, a few pieces of modern art and a twelve-string guitar leaning against an Eames Chair in worn leather—all things that, if her mind-set had been different, she'd have regarded as intriguing evidence of the private man.

After splashing cold water on her face in his tiny bathroom, she emerged to find Aaron clinking ice into a pair of glasses. While she'd been freshening up, he'd taken off his shoes and changed to shorts and a faded T-shirt. The shorts exposed lean, well-muscled thighs. Kendra felt impossibly overdressed in her tightly laced oxfords and nurse's uniform.

"Scotch all right?" he asked.

"I'm not much for alcohol."

He grinned. "One drink won't hurt. Tonight it's just what the doctor ordered."

Picking up their glasses, he led her to a small screened lanai overlooking the water. They sat at opposite ends of a rusty glider upholstered with faded cushions in a tropical print. Accepting her Scotch, Kendra raised the glass to her lips. Though Aaron had diluted the alcohol with water, it was still much stronger than she'd expected. She sputtered, bringing a smile to his face.

"Easy does it," he recommended, setting the glider into motion. "No need to gulp and run. I'm always wired after a day at the hospital and it'll be therapeutic for me to sit and listen. That is, if you think talking would help."

Kendra didn't answer him for a moment. Lulled by the glider's gentle motion and his undemanding presence, she allowed her anguish to surface. When they came this time, her tears were a silent river, streaming down her cheeks.

Wordlessly he covered her free hand with his. For some reason the gesture overcame her reticence to speak. Haltingly at first, because every word was painful, she poured out the whole sorry tale of Glenn's death and the letter that had subsequently broken the news of his defection.

My God, Aaron thought, his heart going out to her. How awful she must feel. Separately, widowhood and learning of a mate's infidelity were enough to make a person go around the bend. Together...! He shook his head. He wished he could think of something to say that would help. But he couldn't. He didn't want to respond with pity. Or encourage her sense of being victimized.

"I know this sort of thing happens to other women, too," she added when he didn't speak. "It's just that I feel so...*used.* As if Glenn made a fool of me...."

Aaron's dark brows lifted perceptibly at that. "Rotten things happen to nice people," he answered. "But no one can make a fool of you unless you let them. Isn't there something you'd like to do with the rest of your life?"

Tossed out without preliminaries, the query startled her. Taking another sip of her Scotch, Kendra stared at him. "Actually, there *is* something I've always wanted to do.... Something my husband actively discouraged," she admitted. "I'd like to go to medical school."

Unlike Glenn, Aaron didn't laugh or discourage her. "Why?" he asked matter-of-factly, as if people contemplated climbing that particular mountain every day.

Kendra shrugged. She hadn't mentioned her inability to have a child and the aching emptiness that made her feel. Hence, he wouldn't understand why a career in pediatric medicine was the best contribution she could imagine herself making to the next generation—especially youngsters who might otherwise have to do without competent medical help.

"If I were a doctor, I'd use my knowledge to aid the disadvantaged," she said.

Enthusiasm leaped in his eyes. "If you feel that way," he said, their tawny depths gleaming at her in the shadows, "you shouldn't let anything stop you. People willing to make that kind of contribution are rare."

Swirling the ice in her glass, Kendra didn't answer.

"What makes you think you couldn't do it?" he said.

She shrugged again. "The cost, for one thing. And I'm not sure I could do the work. True, I have my B.S. in nursing and that includes basic anatomy, biology and chemistry. But I'm lacking a number of advanced science credits...."

He rolled his eyes. "Get them, then! Everybody's got to start somewhere. As for your brain power, I'm willing to bet it's more than adequate. Didn't what's-his-name leave you any money?"

By now Kendra was swimming in a pleasant, alcohol-induced haze. "I have a military pension, of course, since I didn't have time to divorce Glenn," she acknowledged. "It would pay my living expenses. And there are the proceeds from several insurance policies. But, under the circumstances, I'm not sure I'd want to touch a penny of that..."

"You little ninny...."

Despite her inebriated state, Kendra was astute enough to take the epithet as a compliment. The heady feeling it imparted was short-lived.

"What about your husband's girlfriend?" Aaron asked. "And her unborn child? Are they provided for?"

The question hit her where it hurt the most. "I don't know," she shot back, stung. "They're not my responsibility!"

A moment later she wanted to throttle herself. It didn't matter what Aaron thought; she didn't owe him an explanation. But she was deeply ashamed that, in allowing her raw emotions to surface, she'd laid the blame for her hurt and disillusionment on an innocent child.

Somehow, I'll have to find Glenn's lover and make sure their baby is adequately cared for, she thought. Maybe I can hire an attorney to seek her out. She doubted if she could bear to face the woman herself.

Aaron didn't push. It's only normal she should feel as she does, he thought. She's been hurt, and badly. Given time, she'll heal. He didn't question that, ultimately, she'd do what was right.

A half hour later he was shaking her by the shoulders. "Where...?" she asked, blinking at the unfamiliar setting.

"My apartment." There was an amused expression on his face. "C'mon... I'm putting you to bed."

Her eyes focused fully at his words. "You mean... here?"

"You're in no condition to pick up your car. And there's no reason why you can't stay here...."

"I'm not drunk! I've never been drunk in my life!" Struggling to her feet, Kendra had trouble maintaining her balance. Her legs felt as if they were made of rubber.

Gently Aaron took hold of her elbow. She was so funny and appealing, this bereft, proud and feisty redhead. He wanted to shelter her in his arms.

"Look," he said, leading her to a small bedroom that was sparsely furnished with a dresser and double bed. "Don't be too hard on yourself. Most people would do more than down a little Scotch with the emotional load you're carrying."

Worse for the wear though she was, it struck her that he was giving up his bed. "Please," she protested, attempting to back out of the room. "I can't put you out."

"I don't see why not. I've fallen asleep on the couch in front of the television many times."

Lacking the will to argue, Kendra sank down on the coverlet. Clumsily she tried to untie her shoelaces.

He bent to help. "Stand up and turn around," he ordered a moment later. "I'll unzip your dress."

He was a doctor, after all. He'd seen lots of women in their underthings. Yet she avoided his eyes as she slithered out of her uniform and white nylon panty hose, and unpinned her hair so that it fell, an awkwardly waving mass, about her shoulders.

Aaron wanted to lift it, let its texture and weight spill through his fingers. But it wasn't the time even if it might someday be the place. Before she got involved with anyone new, her spirit needed to heal. And he was too much of a gentleman to take advantage of her vulnerable state.

"Now then," he said, steadying her with impersonal hands. "Will that slip be all right to sleep in? Or would you like a shirt?"

"The slip'll be fine. But really..."

"Go on, then. Get into bed. I've got surgery in the morning. We can't stand here discussing this all night."

His tone sharper than he'd intended, he gave her shoulders a little squeeze. "Here," he added. "I'll even pull back the bedcovers."

Settling her against the pillows, Aaron switched off the lamp. "Good night," he said, pausing in the half-light from the doorway. "Sleep well."

When he'd squeezed her shoulders, Kendra had wanted to snuggle like a kitten or a puppy against his chest. "Aaron?" she asked, unconsciously availing herself of his given name.

"Yes?"

The Scotch was still buzzing in her head and he had to wait a moment while she framed her answer. "I feel like a fool for asking," she said at last. "But I need to be close to someone tonight. Do you suppose you could..."

"Stay here with you?"

She nodded, suddenly too shy to speak.

His hazel eyes unreadable, Aaron considered her request. Deciding he could handle the situation, he stripped quickly to his shorts and turned off the other lights in the apartment. Moments later the mattress shifted as he got in beside her. Kendra felt herself being drawn against the muscular warmth of his body.

To her astonishment, his mouth brushed her forehead in a light yet incredibly tender kiss. "Close your eyes, Kendra Jenkins," he whispered, his voice a throaty growl that comforted her like a blanket. "Forget everything that hurts and just go to sleep."

Chapter One

Six years later, as she drove back to St. Petersburg to begin the final phase of her medical education, Kendra recalled the night she and Aaron Dash had spent together. That was a long time ago, she thought, glancing at the dull sheen of Tampa Bay beneath a cloudy sky. He's probably forgotten it. Yet for her, as she returned to Children's Memorial for her residency, the emotions that had flowed from their bittersweet encounter were as poignant as yesterday.

Funny, she didn't feel the slightest bit nostalgic or uneasy over seeing the haunts she'd once frequented with Glenn—just about meeting the amber-eyed physician who'd sheltered her in his bed. Will it jog his memory when my name turns up on the list of residents assigned to him? she wondered. Maybe if I mentioned a sobbing nurse who got pie-eyed on a single jolt of Scotch and spilled her guts in his apartment it would ring a bell.

During her years at the University of Florida Medical School in Gainesville, she'd focused on Glenn less and less. Yct the sight of a young Asian woman or child still made her think of the child born after his death. Despite several attempts, the attorney who'd settled Glenn's estate had failed to locate the woman named Arn Song. And, though Kendra couldn't seem to shake off her jealousy of the mistress who'd borne the child she felt *she* should have had, she regretted her inability to provide for that child's welfare.

Now that I'll be living in the Tampa Bay area again, I'll have him give it another try, she thought. If we can find Glenn's baby, it deserves to benefit from its father's estate.

Time and the pressure of Kendra's studies hadn't obviated her frustrated desire to be a mother. She wondered if she'd ever come to terms with it. The emptiness she felt wasn't likely to be filled unless she adopted as a single parent someday. Unlike Glenn, she guessed, most men wanted children—their *own* children. And that was something she could never give a husband. Working with youngsters day in and day out had become her substitute. It brought her tremendous satisfaction, though it had the effect, too, of keeping her yearning alive.

Meanwhile, Aaron had continued to occupy her thoughts at odd moments. It was curious how the scent and sound and feel of a man she'd known only briefly had clung to her through so much mind-numbing work. In her fantasies he'd become her mentor, giving her the praise and you-can-do-it pep talks she'd never received from anyone but deeply craved. He'd even aimed one or two imaginary kicks at her derriere on those few occasions when she'd thought about abandoning her quest.

But she hadn't seen him exclusively in that role. Sometimes, when she'd cracked the books until she thought her brain would melt, she'd stretched out exhausted on her narrow bed in the medical students' residence hall and let her mind wander. Inevitably on those occasions her longing for the love and closeness other women enjoyed had surfaced. Whenever it had, Aaron's was always the face she saw, his the body she ached to feel curling protectively around hers in sleep.

She supposed it was just one of those things. Though she'd been emotionally upset the night they'd spent together and not really interested in him as a man, since then her interest had grown. Perhaps that was because there'd been no one special in her life. Except for a few occasions, she'd been too preoccupied with her studies to date.

Whatever the case, she certainly hadn't come back to Children's Memorial expecting a love affair. Even if that had seemed like a possibility—which it didn't—she knew they'd never be able to pursue it. Professors simply didn't get involved with residents. She found herself hoping time had changed him, making him less attractive than she remembered.

Kendra doubted she'd made a similarly strong impression on him. On that long-ago morning when she'd awakened in his bed, he'd already gone. Instead of opening her eyes to the wry grin that was probably characteristic of him away from the hospital, she'd been greeted by his car keys and a note informing her that he'd hitched a ride to work.

"Try tomato juice with a raw egg if coffee and aspirin don't work," he'd written in his atrocious physician's scrawl. "No thank-yous are necessary. You can leave the keys in my box at the hospital."

She'd felt a distinct twinge of loss. Well, why should his tone be anything but impersonal? she asked herself. We're nothing to each other. I'm just your basic stray cat he dragged in from the rain.

She hadn't seen him again after that night. After driving home to her Tampa apartment to shower and change after switching cars, she'd returned to the hospital, sought out Bess Martin and invoked emergency leave. A week later Kendra had quit her job and enrolled in the courses she required to get into medical school.

Now fate was closing the circle, completing the gestalt. It was bringing her back to the starting place. Out of the blue, Dr. Ed Burford, her adviser at UF, had recommended Aaron and Children's Memorial for her chosen specialty. Besieged by feelings she hadn't examined too closely, she'd decided to apply. And the committee at Children's had accepted her application. Though her residency wouldn't begin for nearly three weeks, she had an appointment that afternoon with Dr. Bertrand Ames, director of the Children's Memorial-University of South Florida residency program.

"Well, Kendra!" Dr. Ames growled heartily, a pleased smile on his face as he welcomed her into his office. "This is a genuine pleasure, my dear. Except for the M.D. after your name and all that fancy knowledge they stuffed into your head up at Gainesville, you haven't changed a bit!"

Kendra returned his smile with interest. "I hope that's a compliment, doctor," she said.

"You know it is." He patted her shoulder. "Sit down, sit down, we have a lot to talk about. You've chosen a very demanding program and, as I'm sure you know, an exacting mentor. But your credentials are excellent. Ed Burford tells me your internship at Shands was outstanding. And if I remember correctly, you're an extremely hard worker. I'm sure you'll do very well."

"Thanks. I appreciate the vote of confidence."

Giving her a benevolent look, Dr. Ames launched into a discussion of the hospital's pediatric program. "When it comes to pediatric cardiology these days," he concluded, "Aaron Dash is among the best in his field. I'm sure I needn't tell you he can be very precise, especially where patient welfare is concerned. But I think I can guarantee one thing—your diligence and dedication won't go unrewarded."

From experience, Kendra was inclined to agree—both about Aaron's toughness and his decency. She knew measuring up to his standards wouldn't be easy. But the really hard part, she guessed, might turn out to be keeping her wayward imagination under control. During her six years away from St. Petersburg, she hadn't met the man who could compare with him.

"I'm looking forward to the challenge," she answered.

"Excellent!" Getting to his feet, the good doctor consulted a schedule. "As a matter of fact, Aaron's operating now," he informed her. "Shall we have a look?"

On their way upstairs, Dr. Ames explained that the afternoon's procedure would attempt to repair a baby's congenitally malformed heart. It was delicate, risk-filled surgery. Aaron and his team were using a relatively new technique.

Despite her resolve to be sensible, Kendra's heart beat a little faster when they stepped into the small observation gallery, which overlooked the operating theater through a thick wall of glass. Beyond it, surrounded by a battery of lights and equipment, a tightly knit group of men and women bent over their tiny patient. The public address system sometimes used to provide commentary for medical students was turned off. As familiar as Kendra was by now with surgical technique, the action surrounding the operating table reminded her of a taut drama in pantomime.

Swallowing hard, she approached the window. She couldn't see very much of the actual surgery itself. Several physicians were taking part, all of them male, fairly tall and dressed in the usual green surgical garb. Though his dark hair and most of his face were hidden by his cap and mask, she recognized Aaron instantly. Muscular and spare in his wrinkled scrubs, he was at the center of the tense, carefully controlled battle to repair the baby's heart. Her lips parting softly, she noted the way his powerful biceps flexed slightly as he worked. Every line of his body, every gesture, spelled concentration.

Unfortunately for her peace of mind, the memories she'd carried for so long were no match for the man himself. *He* was the Rembrandt, they the paltry imitation. Separated from him by a wall of glass and more than half a decade, she could almost smell his clean, spicy man-scent, hear the low growl of his voice telling her to go to sleep.

Gooseflesh spread like a ripple of longing over her skin. What a beautiful man he is! she exclaimed silently, overcome by the reality of him. And what an amalgam of opposites! Demanding but fair. Uncompromising and tender. If there's a woman in his life, I truly envy her.

As they watched, Aaron gave a satisfied nod and started to close. It looked as if the operation would be a success. Seconds later Kendra was gripped with unreasoning panic as he glanced up to speak with his anesthesiologist. The man was standing with his back to them and, for the space of a heartbeat, Aaron's gaze moved past him to the gallery window. Above the surgical mask his light-drenched eyes held a surprised, almost questioning look. A split second later his attention had snapped back to the child on the table.

I doubt if he actually *saw* us, Kendra thought, getting hold of herself. If I know him at all, Aaron's much too focused as a surgeon to pay any real heed to the gallery even though they're just mopping up. Yet she'd been staring at him—hard. Had he felt the intrusiveness of her gaze?

Weak-kneed at the prospect of working in close proximity with him, she followed Dr. Ames out into the hall. Mercifully the latter didn't appear to notice her state of mind. His invitation to accompany him on brief rounds helped to restore her perspective.

They're the reason I'm here, not Aaron, Kendra reminded herself as she chatted with a succession of youthful patients who were recuperating or awaiting surgery by one of the staff specialists. When my residency's finished, I'll be leaving St. Petersburg, carrying what I've learned to underprivileged children in some isolated spot on the globe. He'll be just a memory once again.

She thought immediately of Glenn's son or daughter and, as a consequence, her own unfortunate inability to have children when Dr. Ames introduced her to a boy he said was Aaron's star patient. A thin, handsome youngster with coal black hair and large, beautiful eyes, ten-year-old Cambodian refugee Sem Troon gave her a shy smile.

He's older than Glenn's child, she thought, returning it and shaking hands with the boy. The baby he had with Song must be the right age for kindergarten now. I can't help wishing he or she could have been mine.

Though he appeared eager to make friends, Sem Troon couldn't speak any English. He was in traction for a broken leg.

"What's he doing here in St. Petersburg?" Kendra asked. "I thought most of the Southeast Asians in this area lived in Tampa. And why is he on the cardiology unit?"

Dr. Ames prepared to listen to Troon's heart with the aid of his stethoscope. "We have quite a few Vietnamese and Cambodians on this side of the bay now," he said after a moment. "Most of the latter are fairly recent arrivals and decidedly low income. Troon happens to be an orphan. He presented with a compound fracture in the emergency room. The woman who'd been caring for him said he fell through the rotted wood railing of a second-story porch."

Kendra waited as Dr. Ames took the boy's pulse.

"Though the fracture was serious," he added, patting Troon's head, "we quickly discovered that his most critical problem was a seriously undersized aortic valve in his heart. He's also got a defective sinus node. Aaron will be operating soon to enlarge the valve and install a dual-chamber, rate-responsive pacemaker. Unfortunately, the boy's diet has been inadequate for years, making him a poor risk for such extensive surgery. While his leg is healing, we're trying to build up his reserves."

At last they were back in Dr. Ames's office. "Well, my dear," he said, taking Kendra's hand firmly in his, "that's our cardiology setup in a nutshell. I've very glad you've come back to us. Please let me know if there's anything—"

Before he could finish there was a rap on his office door. "Come in," he responded, glancing over the top of his half glasses at the source of interruption.

Kendra caught her breath as Aaron strode into the room. He was still wearing his scrubs and his hair was disheveled from the cap he'd just removed. "A little while ago, while I was in surgery—" he began and then stopped in midsentence.

Though it was a woman's prerogative to remain seated, Kendra got to her feet. "Hello, Dr. Dash," she said tentatively, the words far huskier than she'd intended.

For a moment he simply stared. She's even more special than I remembered, he thought, taking her in from head to toe. Skin smooth as cream, with freckles scattered lightly over it as if she were some billionairess who could afford to powder her nose with gold dust. How well I remember the way those big green eyes of hers can glint with suppressed anger, yet seem completely vulnerable the next moment. She has hair like a Titian Madonna. Or a barbarian princess. And that mouth... How had he managed to keep from kissing it on that night so long ago?

The silence between them was becoming a little awkward. "So you're back," he said finally, his deep, nubby-as-tweed voice faintly clipped.

Surrounding herself with poise like a fortress, she nodded. "I suppose you've heard. It's *Dr.* Jenkins now."

"Indeed I have. Congratulations."

As they continued to look at each other, another conversation was going on in the silence—one Kendra didn't dare translate into words. For several seconds it was as if Dr. Ames didn't exist.

"I was very pleased to learn you'd gone ahead with medical school...and that you'll be one of my residents," Aaron added. "I got the list a couple of weeks ago."

Usually quick on the uptake, Kendra couldn't think of a single thing to say. Seeing him again had all but robbed her of the capacity for intelligent speech. She hoped Dr. Ames wouldn't decide she was behaving like an idiot.

Yet she could hardly blame herself. Seen at close range, the man who'd come to her rescue that night in the parking lot was everything she remembered and then some. The years they'd been apart had been kind to him, merely etching the attractive creases that framed his mouth slightly deeper and sprinkling a handful of silver at his temples. Though he exuded the same wired, full-tilt energy, he'd acquired a distinguished look.

Physically he was at the peak of his form, his broad shoulders and powerful arms obviously conditioned by exercise. She couldn't detect an inch of flab at his narrow waist or flat midsection. What would it be like, she wondered, to see that taut, muscular body react to the throes of passion, those topaz eyes go smoky with desire?

"Yes, well . . ." With a little shrug that was infinitely more casual than she felt, Kendra gathered up her purse. "I wanted the best. Not an easy ride."

A little curve of his mouth acknowledged the backhanded compliment. He could laugh at himself; it made his demanding, perfectionist side easier to forgive. She had the sudden feeling they could sit and talk as they once had, without Scotch or the stimulus of an emotional crisis, and the years would just melt away. They'd still be able to communicate as if they'd always known each other.

The very idea of it frightened her. Our night together was a moment carved out of time, she thought. Reality was suspended for the duration. If you became intimate with him now, your willpower and your residency would self-destruct. Abruptly she picked up her purse.

"Thanks for the tour and your good wishes, Dr. Ames," she said as breezily as she could. "I'm looking forward to being in the program . . . and to working with you, Dr. Dash."

Aaron nodded, though he didn't speak. He looked as if he had several questions on the tip on his tongue—questions he'd have asked but for Dr. Ames's presence.

"Must you go?" the older man protested, seemingly unaware of the undercurrents between them. "I was about to invite you for coffee in the surgeons' lounge."

She gave him a regretful smile. "I really should. Besides, the two of you probably have a lot to discuss. See you both in two and a half weeks."

On her way to Kim Johanssen's house, where she'd be staying until she located an apartment, Kendra couldn't get Aaron out of her mind. Seeing him again so suddenly had been like awakening from a lengthy nap to find the real world more delicious, more captivating than one remembered. Just by walking into the room, he'd called forth that part of her that was quintessentially female, secretly erotic and more deeply dedicated to giving, bonding and loving than to professional concerns.

She wanted to kick herself for being so susceptible. Use your head, she told herself as she parked in front of the charmingly landscaped bungalow Kim shared with her husband in the city's Old Northeast section. As your residency professor, Aaron Dash is out of reach. Besides, he isn't interested in you as a woman.

A moment later she was wishing she'd noticed whether he was wearing a wedding band.

Removing her suitcases from the hatchback's cargo space, Kendra mounted the bungalow's front steps. If anyone could be counted on to drive the past and Aaron from her mind, she knew it was Kim. Following the incident in which Kendra had covered for her former assistant, the two of them had become friends. Kim had visited her in Gainesville several times. Her bubbly, chatty letters about life at Children's Memorial, a bright spot during Kendra's sojourn at medical school, had occasionally contained an added bonus—she'd mentioned Aaron, most often in the form of a good-natured complaint.

Kendra was about to ring the bell when Kim threw open the front door with a flourish and held out her arms. "Kendra . . . how marvelous!" she exclaimed. "I can't believe you're really here at last!"

"Neither can I." Dropping her bags, Kendra returned Kim's hug.

"Don't just stand there . . . come in!" her friend demanded. "You look terrific! How are you, anyway? Smart as a whip, filled to the brim with knowledge and ready to take on our resident dragon, I suppose?"

Kendra pretended to shudder. "You mean Aaron Dash, of course."

"Who else? He thinks the *D* in M.D. stands for 'deity,' or so I'm told!"

Leaving the suitcases in the foyer, they linked arms and went into the living room. "So tell me," Kim teased. "Now that you're one of *them,* do I have to bow and scrape, or what?"

Kendra couldn't help laughing at the outrageous dig. Her friend's marriage to one of *them,* namely Dr. Dan Johanssen, was a very happy one. "Hardly," she responded. "I'm sure you know that residents are still grubs when it comes to the pecking order."

They regarded each other fondly for a moment.

"Is he married?" Kendra asked without thinking. Seconds later she wanted to clap her hand over her mouth.

At first Kim stared as if she hadn't heard correctly. "You mean Aaron?" she said at last.

"Umm, yes . . . I guess that's what I *do* mean," Kendra admitted, feeling a flush spread over her cheeks.

"Nope. Confirmed bachelor." Kim made a face. "Don't tell me you've got the hots for him!"

"I wouldn't put it like that!"

Thoroughly embarrassed, Kendra wished she'd never raised the subject. Yet even as her flush deepened, she felt a lovely glow of relief in the vicinity of her heart.

Though her own introduction to Aaron six years before had been less than fortuitous, Kim had a reputation for fairness. "You could do a lot worse," she said thoughtfully, without a hint of teasing in her eyes.

Chapter Two

As she and Kim sipped a couple of soft drinks, traded gossip and made plans to go to the beach, Kendra let her relief permeate blood and bone. Aaron was single. He hadn't pledged a lifetime of love and devotion to anyone.

You're crazy, she said to herself as her friend's phone rang and Kim went into the other room to answer it. Whatever his plans for the rest of his life, they don't include you. Get that into your head and keep it there. You're here to work and to learn, period. When your residency is over, you won't see him again.

Kim returned shaking her head. "Can you believe it?" she asked. "I take a couple of days off, hoping the two of us can bum around together. So naturally my sister has to go into early labor. The baby was born an hour ago. It's her first and I promised to fly to Cleveland on Saturday. Dan will probably go with me if he can get away, since we're supposed to be godparents. After extending our hospitality, it looks like we'll be leaving you here all alone."

As always, the mention of someone having a baby struck a bittersweet chord in Kendra's heart. "That's okay," she said, smiling at her friend. "I'm going to be around for a while. What did your sister have? A boy or a girl?"

At the hospital, Aaron was concluding his rounds in Sem Troon's room. A fluent speaker of Khmer, the Cambodian language, which he'd learned during military duty in Thailand, he sat on the edge of the young refugee's bed and quizzed him about his day. In the process of answering, Troon described two visitors: Dr. Ames and a tall American lady with bright, beautiful hair.

Aaron pricked up his ears at the description. So Kendra had stopped in to see his favorite patient. What had she thought of Troon? he wondered. Had she felt drawn, as he did, by the boy's quiet bravery, the cheerful way he endured discomfort—even after a life of turmoil and deprivation?

"What did they talk about?" he asked in Troon's native tongue.

"I don't know, Dr. Dash," the boy answered. *"They spoke in English. I couldn't understand."*

Absently he ruffled Troon's hair. Damn, but I wish I didn't have to fly to Miami in the morning, he thought. I'd call her and we'd go out for a pizza or something—just to talk. I don't see how that could be against the rules.

Of course, he didn't know where Kendra was staying. And Bert Ames might find it odd if he asked for her phone number. But there were other ways of finding out. He'd be back on Saturday. Maybe then . . .

He'd been telling her the literal truth about how pleased he was to find her name on a computer printout of new residents assigned to him. So she went and did it! he'd exclaimed. More power to her! He felt a small glow of pride, thinking that perhaps something he'd said or done the night she'd spent in his apartment had given her the extra push she needed.

Probably it was too much to expect, but he couldn't help wishing she'd seen fit to contact him at some point during her absence. He'd cultivated a soft spot for her, just as he'd always taken a shine to tall, sexy redheads.

Standing now in Troon's room, he made appropriate noises as the boy chatted about a visit he'd had earlier in the day. Morng Ny, the Cambodian woman who'd been caring for Troon and another orphan, Dith Lin, had brought the younger boy to visit via the city bus. In an act of heroism that could have jeopardized their own chance to emigrate, Ny and her husband, Houm, had smuggled both boys out of a displaced persons camp in Thailand to a new home in the United States by claiming them as their own children.

Though the boys were unrelated, they'd become fast friends, creating a sort of family for each other. By now, their status as legal aliens in the United States was secure. Yet Aaron feared their current home situation would prove a temporary one.

Ny had become pregnant and she wasn't doing very well. In addition, she and her husband were trying to make a go of a struggling restaurant in a run-down section on the city's south side. So far they were earning barely enough to make ends meet without two extra mouths to feed. Even if they could find a way to keep Lin, he suspected they'd never be able to make the huge investment of time, energy and money Troon was going to need. And they were too proud to take very much in the way of help.

It would be a tragedy of the first order, he thought, noting the sparkle in Troon's dark eyes as he talked about Lin's visit, for the two of them to become separated. They spent time in the refugee camp together. Each provides the other with a tie to his past.

Aaron wanted to adopt them both. He was single but that didn't matter these days. Or so he'd thought. He was a decent human being and a good citizen—he hadn't even had a traffic ticket in years. What was more, he spoke the boys' language. He could afford to hire a housekeeper and pay for whatever medical help Troon required.

Most importantly of all, he *cared* about them. It wasn't just the debt he felt to the ragtag bunch of children who'd saved his life in Vietnam.

Determined to show he could provide stability and a suitable home, he'd given up his cozy bachelor apartment for a rambling two-story craftsman-style house facing Coffee Pot Bayou across a rosy brick street. Built in 1925, the house had a vaguely oriental feel with its slightly peaked roof and trellised carport. There was a veritable rain forest of tropical vegetation out back and it was large enough that each boy would have his own room, with a separate room for Aaron and one for guests left over. The place even boasted a detached garage with an upstairs apartment for the housekeeper he intended to hire.

His hopes soaring like a kite, he'd run smack into a stone wall at the Kampuchean Christian Children's Relief Association, Inc. The officials of KCCRA were sympathetic but adamant on one immutable point. Without exception, orphans who entered the country under their aegis were adopted into two-parent families. That was their policy. It reflected the Christian ideal of mother, father and child that was modeled on the family of Bethlehem.

"I know our rules must seem archaic and unbending to you," the director had told him regretfully. "And that you'd do your best to be a good father to the boys. But we have to think of our children first. They've been through a great deal and they're entitled to the warmth and security only a two-parent family can provide."

In an obvious attempt to reassure him, the man had gone on to say that finding families for the orphans in the association's charge hadn't proved all that difficult.

Maybe not, Aaron had countered silently—at least where healthy youngsters are concerned. But what about Troon? His heart condition is going to need constant monitoring as he grows up, even if our surgery is successful. Will the family that adopts Lin be willing to take on that kind of burden?

"Supposing you do find the perfect couple to take the boys," he'd argued. "What if, next month or next year, one of the adoptive partners dies? Or the couple gets a divorce? Would the absence of one parent make the other any less fit to raise a child? If not, why can't a qualified single parent make a home for them?"

Admitting that no one could predict the future, the man had refused to budge an inch. If Lin is adopted and Troon isn't, Troon will die of loneliness and abandonment, Aaron thought now in Troon's hospital room. He gave the boy's thin shoulders a little squeeze.

Returning home to a largely empty house and a solitary meal of frozen burritos heated in the microwave, he continued to think about Kendra in the context of Lin and Troon. What if she weren't one of my residents and I were free to court her? he asked himself. How would she feel about my plan to adopt two orphan boys?

By now, he was certain, Kendra had gotten over her late husband's treachery and learned to trust again. But even if circumstances would allow them to have the kind of relationship he sensed they could build together, she was just starting her career. She might not be anxious to take on a ready-made family. Most women looked forward to having children of their own and, for a busy doctor, one or two youngsters might be enough. Would the thought of raising two needy orphans drive her away before he had half a chance?

Hell, he told himself in disgust, finishing a soft drink and crumpling the can as a way of venting his frustration. You don't have a thing to worry about. The relief association isn't going to let you have the boys. And, in your position as Kendra's professor of record, you have no business getting involved with her. Yet he knew himself. What he wanted, he usually got—eventually. Maybe if she's still speaking to me when her residency is finished I'll have a chance with her, he thought.

His seriousness about a woman he didn't know well surprised him a little. But not that much. Something extraordinary had happened when their paths had crossed on that balmy summer night. He'd gotten close to a woman he found extremely attractive, and discovered the attraction wasn't just physical. Instinctively he'd wanted to shelter her from life's bumps and bruises even while he egged on her fighting spirit.

With Kendra, there hadn't been any of the usual posturing or need to strip away layers of pretense that he hated. The real person she was had been there from the beginning, shining in her big green eyes.

When she'd disappeared, quitting her job at the hospital six years earlier, no doubt one of the nurses on her former unit could have given him her new address and phone number. For some reason—the pressure of his work, perhaps, or his habit of not getting too involved with anyone—he hadn't asked for it. And he'd regretted it, after it had seemed too late.

Now he was thirty-eight and tired of bachelorhood. He wanted a woman and a family to love. Despite the formidable barrier of professional ethics, he found himself paying close attention to an inner voice that whispered, *Don't let her slip through your fingers again.*

Kim's husband got a few stares when he arrived at the airport on Saturday with a blonde on one arm and a redhead on the other. "Tell me what kind of after-shave you use, man," the baggage handler said with a grin. "I wanna get me some."

With half an hour remaining until departure time, they found seats in the waiting area. At last the Johanssens' plane was ready to take off for Cleveland. "We'll be back in a week at most," Kim reminded her, giving Kendra a hug. "Hold down the fort and don't forget to feed the parrot, okay? Be sure to help yourself to anything in the refrigerator."

Kendra's mouth curved. "Don't worry... Polly will get her cracker. And so will I. Give the baby a kiss for me."

A moment later Kim and her husband were disappearing down the jetway. Suddenly feeling very alone, Kendra elected not to wait until their flight took off. I've still got fifteen days before the salt mines crank up, she thought. I might as well go home, change and head for the beach. I won't have much chance for that sort of thing once my residency starts.

Turning to go, she ran squarely into a hard masculine chest. Instantly her nerve endings telegraphed their awareness of hard muscle beneath a white cotton polo shirt. Crisp chest hair poking through its open neck tickled her nostrils. A pair of firm hands steadied her by the shoulders.

"Excuse me," she murmured, disengaging herself as she inhaled a tangy, breezy scent. "I'm afraid I wasn't looking where I was going."

The next moment her heart was constricting and the words were faltering in her throat. No. It can't be, she thought, letting reality sink in. Thanks to a capricious fate, she'd bumped straight into Aaron Dash. There was no fatherly Dr. Ames on hand to mediate.

"Well," Aaron saluted her, a flicker of incredulity lighting his eyes. "I didn't count on running into *you* this afternoon."

Who could have imagined the possibility?

"I just put Kim and Dan Johanssen on a plane for Cleveland," she said, feeling a need to explain herself. "No doubt you know them. What are you doing at the airport?"

He grinned. "They haven't placed it off-limits to me yet. Actually, I'm just returning from a two-day medical conference in Miami."

"Oh. I see."

Neither of them said anything more for a moment. The light pressure of his fingertips sent little shivers of pleasure down her bare arms.

We actually spent a whole night together, Kendra reminded herself, stunned. In his bed. Wearing only our underwear. Despite the airport bustle swirling around them, the barriers imposed by her residency and their lack of an extensive history together, she wanted to throw her arms about his neck.

She's marvelous, Aaron thought. Even more of a woman than I remembered. And it's not just a surface thing. There's a resonance, a hard-won depth about her she'd only begun to acquire six years ago.

Instead of a business suit and pumps, she was wearing flat sandals and a white piqué sundress that made her look about twenty. She smelled like a field full of lilies. Unbound, her hair was a copper halo, blazoning the air. Here, today, at this very moment, he decided, she's the most perfect peach on the tree. Though I'm about to become her professor, I'll be damned if any other man is going to get her first.

He wasn't sure how he could prevent it. Realizing neither of them had moved or spoken for almost a minute, he released her. She gave a little sigh.

"I take it you drove to the airport," he said, seizing a way to spend some time with her.

Still half-mesmerized by his nearness, she nodded.

"How about giving me a lift back across the bay, then? If you don't, I'll have to take the limo. And we have a lot of catching up to do."

She could hardly refuse. In point of fact, she didn't *want* to—even if being alone with him was too emotionally risky to think about. She felt like she was being pushed out of a plane without getting her parachute properly fastened first. She didn't know where she might land. Or even if she'd survive the fall.

I want to be with him, she thought. Even if there *is* a risk involved. At least we'll have a few unharried moments together before the madness starts.

"I'd be happy to," she said as casually as she could. "Can I help you carry anything?"

"Thanks, no. I've just got this garment bag."

He fell into step beside her, his long legs, bared by khaki shorts and lightly furred with the dark body hair she remembered, easily matching her usual brisk pace. He was dressed much as he'd been that night in his apartment, with the exception of his polo shirt and rope-soled canvas shoes. He looked tanned, breezy and confident. And, oh, so delicious to hold.

She didn't know what to say to him on the people mover that shuttled between the main terminal and the gates. Fortunately there were quite a few other passengers so it wasn't necessary to make conversation.

The brief hiatus gave her a chance to think. On her way back to St. Petersburg, she'd yearned to look her fill at his tall, muscular frame and light-drenched eyes. She'd even fantasized fate might throw them together. But she'd never really expected anything like that to happen. All her real energy had been focused on her career.

Now that he was a flesh-and-blood reality standing less than a foot away from her, things had become infinitely more complex. She'd begun to think of him as a man, not a fantasy lover. At the same time, thanks to their professor-student relationship, he seemed even farther out of reach. It's going to be hell, she decided, maintaining a strictly business relationship with him.

He'd said they had a lot of catching up to do. And in a way he was right. As the man who'd encouraged her to become a doctor and the one who'd be her teacher now, he deserved to hear about her adventures in medical school and question her about her future plans. She hoped it would be enough to get them across the bay to wherever he was living now without too much awkwardness.

Kendra's modest import was parked near the red elevators. Though the fifth floor of the garage was crowded with cars, it was virtually empty of people. After stashing his garment bag in the hatchback, Aaron followed her to the driver's side. Gazing down at her, he found her softly parted lips almost impossible to resist.

Somehow he had to harden his heart. But there isn't any law dictating that we can't spend time together, just talking, he convinced himself. Though we're less than friends, we're more than acquaintances. Her residency hasn't even started yet.

"How about dinner tonight?" he asked. "Feel free to say no if you've got other plans."

Kendra jumped as if he'd suggested a trip to the moon. Coming from out of the blue, his invitation had chased every coherent thought from her head.

"The truth is, I haven't," she confessed. "Any other plans, that is. But I don't think..."

They seemed to have moved a little closer together. "Why not?" he asked, his voice almost a whisper, though there wasn't the slightest chance they'd be overheard.

"Our upcoming association at the hospital—"

"Doesn't start for a couple of weeks. Meanwhile, I don't see how it could hurt for us to share a meal and reminisce."

They had only one memory in common. The thought of discussing it with him was so intimate a little thrill of anticipation raced down her spine.

Something of what she was feeling must have shown in her face. Though he considered it completely unacceptable to get involved with a woman who'd be dependent on him for training, grades and references, a wild, iconoclastic spirit came over him. Before either of them knew what was happening, he'd lowered his mouth to hers.

Long imagined, his kiss was so rapturous, so overwhelming Kendra wanted to melt in his arms. Nothing about it was brash or rough. Instead he nuzzled her with a sweet hesitance she guessed could deepen to sensuous demand at the slightest provocation. Time poured out like honey—slow, sweet, in harmony with the pull of gravity.

As they lingered there, intoxicated by the scent and feel of each other, she hardly dared to take a breath.

Operating solely on instinct instead of giving himself a chance to think about it, Aaron parted her lips with his tongue. With a little moan, she pressed herself against him.

On the night she'd taken refuge in his bed, his mouth had offered nothing more than compassion, chastely administered to her forehead. She'd been a waif then. A stray cat snatched from a Dumpster. A grown woman crying like a child.

Now, despite the upcoming association that weighed so heavily on both their minds, they were meeting on more equal terms. His capable, exquisitely trained hands were holding out much more than sympathy and shelter. Whole again, she was ready to accept. Finding her way in the rapturous jungle of his kiss, she began to take as well as give. Her tongue dueled and danced with his, imitating that other, far more soul-satisfying partnership that was the theme of every daydream she'd ever had about him.

Aaron's response came from the deepest part of himself. With a little explosion of need, he pulled her closer. Gentleness gave way to passion. Urgency overcame hesitance. It was as if they were making sudden, fevered love there in the hulking concrete parking garage between the dim rows of automobiles.

No stranger in that intimate embrace to how much he wanted her, Kendra felt longing open in her so blatantly that she struggled for breath. To have him kiss her that way, mold her body to his so that she was conversant with every outline of his need, was almost more than she could take. Pressing against his chest through the light barrier of their clothing, her nipples hardened to eager nuggets of readiness. Her pulse hammered like a drumbeat in her ears.

Meshing his fingers in the gleaming curls at her nape, Aaron was stunned at the sense of rightness he felt. What superlative love we could make! he thought. An urge to completion like no other he'd known ricocheted through his blood, giving rise to thoughts of lust and sweet forgetting.

He knew she felt it, too. It sang in the way she caressed him, in her soft, breathless excitement. If—no, *when*—they shared a bed again, neither of them would get any sleep.

The thought brought him up short as if someone had jerked a leash. What the hell do you think you're doing? he asked himself roughly. You know this kind of thing would be against your principles even if it weren't forbidden by formal constraints.

Kendra swayed a little as he let her go. The sudden release precipitated the emotional free-fall she'd pictured earlier and, for a split second, nothing about their surroundings looked even vaguely familiar. Perhaps that was because her heart and mind were still engaged in the passionate embrace that had united them just seconds before.

"Do you curl all the female residents' toes this way?" she stammered, blurting out the first thing that came into her head.

Aaron winced. I deserve that, he thought. And more.

"No, just yours," he said, his hazel eyes shadowed with self-blame. "I don't know what came over me.... Possibly an unfulfilled urge from the past. I'm sorry if I caused you any embarrassment."

"You're...forgiven." Kendra could feel a flush spreading over her cheeks.

Neither of them said anything more for a moment. At last he held out his hand for her car keys and, when she gave them to him, fitted them into the lock.

"After my performance a moment ago, I deserve to hitchhike to St. Petersburg," he said, opening the car door for her. "But I really would like a chance to talk with you. Are you willing to let bygones be bygones and give me a ride?"

Shaken though she was, she wasn't about to tell him no. "Please...get in," she answered. "What happened between us was my fault, too."

They didn't speak again until she'd driven down the ramp and paid her tab at the tollbooth. For her part, Kendra could hardly believe the events of the past few minutes had actually taken place. Is it possible Aaron Dash is really here in the car with me? she asked herself in amazement. Did we just kiss like there's no tomorrow? Or am I back at Kim's house, fast asleep in her guest-room bed?

After the headlong, mindless seconds they'd spent in each other's arms, it seemed the height of incongruity that they could drive calmly away from the airport. They were behaving as if nothing earthshaking had taken place.

"I meant it, you know," he said as they shot into the exit lanes and merged onto Interstate 275.

She threw him a questioning glance.

"That you're the only resident I've ever kissed. I feel like a complete idiot...."

You're not the only one, Kendra thought. Every fantasy I've ever had about you was written all over my face. She could feel her flush returning, hotter than before.

"Please," she said as she concentrated on passing a large truck and semitrailer. "There was no harm done. Do we have to talk about it?"

Perversely, Aaron felt a need to explain. "I just want to make it clear I don't go around doing that sort of thing," he replied. "The trouble is, you're special...."

"I...don't understand."

"There's an old adage. Native American, I think. Or maybe Chinese. It says that when you save a life, it belongs to you. You're responsible for it from that day forward."

"And you think you saved my life?"

He gave her an intense look. "Didn't I?"

For a moment all the loneliness and rage, all the blind seeking for direction that had made her gut ache immediately after getting Glenn's letter were as real as yesterday.

"Yes, you did," she admitted, keeping her eyes on the road, and not just for safety's sake.

Changing the subject, Kendra regaled him with stories about the trials and tribulations of medical school. As she'd hoped, her anecdotes about impossible professors, repeated all-night sessions with the books and, on the plus side, the incomparable satisfaction of learning how to save and improve the lives of children, took them to Aaron's door.

He didn't live in the rather low-key apartment she remembered. Kendra's first impression of his new abode was that it was perfect for a family. Her second was that it needed a little work to bring out all the charm and character it possessed.

"Look," said Aaron as she pulled into the driveway, "we've barely scratched the surface. If you've forgiven me as you said, I'd like to reissue my invitation. I promise I'll behave like your elderly great-uncle and keep my hands to myself."

Aware she should refuse, Kendra wavered. She wasn't ready to say goodbye to him, either. She realized they probably wouldn't have a similar opportunity once her residency got under way.

"How about something that won't put you in a compromising position, like a cheeseburger at Ten Beach Drive?" he added when she didn't speak. "I do need to stop by the hospital for a few minutes first."

Her smile was the answer he'd been hoping for. "Okay," she conceded. "It's a deal. But I ought to warn you.... I don't have a great-uncle. You'll have to play the role by ear."

It's not as if he didn't apologize, she told herself as she sat on his back porch, stirring the glider that had once graced the lanai of his former apartment while she waited for him to change. They were both fully aware that that scene at the airport couldn't be repeated. Yet she knew they'd crossed a Rubicon of sorts. It would be difficult to retreat.

Aaron came back downstairs dressed in cool-looking gray linen slacks and tie, white jacket, light blue shirt. "Ready?" he asked, attempting to strike a casual note. "Why don't we take my car so we can put the top down? It's exactly the right sort of evening to drink the air."

Sadly, the Karmann-Ghia was no more. To replace it, he'd bought a 1965 Fort Mustang convertible and restored it to mint condition. Most of the junk she remembered from the older car—his tennis racquet, sweat socks and beat-up running shoes or at least facsimiles thereof—appeared to have survived the transfer. Seeing it made her feel more at home.

As they drove downtown toward the hospital with the breeze winnowing their hair, Kendra wanted to pinch herself. Beside her was the man she'd imagined was counseling and comforting her every step of the way through the lonely and sometimes frustrating ordeal of medical school.

By some quirk of fate, he gave every indication of being interested in her. Yet thanks to her residency and his place in the scheme of things he was out of rcach.

At least he was while he remained her professor. Unbidden, her thoughts leaped into the future. Next year the rules we have to follow now won't apply, she thought joyously. If he still wants me then, I won't refuse him. For the first time, she began to speculate that the work she planned to do for unfortunate children could be carried out in St. Petersburg.

Kendra was surprised and touched when Aaron's most pressing reason for stopping by the hospital turned out to be Sem Troon, who was still in traction. The boy's face brightened immediately when they stepped into his room.

"Hel-lo, Doc-tor Dash!" he exclaimed, obviously proud that he could greet one of his favorite visitors with a few words in English. Though he smiled at Kendra and appeared to recognize her, it was obvious Aaron was a kind of hero to him.

Placing a hand on the boy's thin shoulder, the man who had so stirred Kendra's soul only a short time before spoke a few rapid words of Khmer. They made the youngster burst into uproarious laughter. He responded happily in the same tongue.

"I told him the nurses complained that he was running up and down the halls, making a nuisance of himself," Aaron translated with a wry grin. "He says he'll behave after this and stay in bed."

Kendra was feeling very warm and approving toward Aaron as they returned to the parking lot. Though Troon's was doubtless a charity case, he clearly viewed it as one of his most important. Despite his occasionally brusque manner, this is a man who loves children and gravitates toward people in need, she thought. Her fantasy future began to take on added color and shape.

She couldn't guess that her lovely house of cards would come tumbling down a few minutes later as they headed for a popular bar and grill situated near St. Petersburg's waterfront.

He broached the topic casually enough.

"Troon and a young friend of his, Dith Lin, are the products of one of the refugee camps that sprang up in Thailand as a result of all the killing in Cambodia during what was known as Pol Pot time—the reign of the Khmer Rouge," he remarked. "They were born there and their parents died there, in an outbreak of dysentery that swept the camp. Right now they're being cared for by a woman called Morng Ny and her husband, Houm, who brought them to the United States. Unfortunately, the Morngs can't afford to keep them much longer. They're not financially able and the wife is having a difficult pregnancy."

Feeling headier and more bemused than she had in years, Kendra didn't sense the land mine that lay in her path. "What will happen to them?" she asked.

Aaron paused a moment before answering. Like her, he'd been thinking of the future and what might happen between them when her residency was finished. Without getting into an overt discussion of the possibilities, he wanted to assure her his intentions regarding Lin and Troon didn't rule out a wish to have children of his own.

"Like most men," he said at last, "I'd like to marry and father a child someday. But in the meantime, I'd like to adopt the boys myself."

Chapter Three

Instant shock and distress registered on Kendra's face. The only man who'd fired her imagination since Glenn's infidelity and death, a man she'd dreamed about all through medical school and suddenly found herself kissing with a splendor that put past experience to shame, wanted a woman who could give him a baby! It was that simple. And that hopeless. Caught up in the magic of seeing him again, she hadn't given the likelihood he would feel that way a second thought.

You should have *known* you could never have him, she thought. Thanks to that stupid accident when you were a kid, you can't give him the fulfillment he deserves.

Too late she tried to hide the anguish she felt. Aaron cursed his own foolhardiness. That makes twice today you've taken a serious misstep with her, he reproached himself. You don't even have the right to court her now. Telling her about the boys was a big mistake.

He didn't blame her for being taken aback at his plans. If she thought of him at all the way he did of her, she had every reason to feel disconcerted. Kids could be a handful. And budding relationships were fragile. New lovers wanted the lion's share of each other's attention. If he succeeded in overcoming the association's objections by the time they were free to see each other, he couldn't promise her anything approaching that.

It was Kendra who spoke first as they pulled into a parking space on Beach Drive. "Can you do that?" she asked, dragging her windblown hair back from her face as she tried to focus on his adoption plans. "I mean, you're single. I know unmarried men and women are being allowed to adopt these days...particularly children like Troon with special needs. Yet you work such long hours. Correct me if I'm wrong, but I have a feeling your whole life has always revolved around medicine. How do you expect to care for them?"

Did she think he was simply looking for someone to help him shoulder the burden of raising the boys? If so, she didn't give any sign of it. A trifle ruefully he admitted the directors of the relief association that had formal custody of them had refused to accept his application because of his single status.

"Naturally, I'm hoping to change their minds," he said. "As for taking care of Troon and Lin, I plan to hire a full-time, live-in housekeeper. It may not be the ideal solution, but it's a damn sight better than some other alternatives I could name. They aren't brothers and the association could decide to split them up...place them in different homes even though they've become close since coming to the United States."

Kendra frowned. "Do you really think that might happen?"

"Sure I do. Lin's a so-called perfect child, highly adoptable. The couple that offers to make a home for him might not be willing to take on a child with Troon's handicaps. Even after we operate on Troon's heart, he'll need close monitoring. There might be a need for further surgery down the line."

"Yet they won't let you have Troon...even if Lin is adopted by someone else?"

He shook his head.

"I think that's very shortsighted of them."

Aaron's eyes hadn't left her face. "So do I," he answered. "I've done everything I can to change the trustees' minds...for instance, buying that house. And offering to set up a trust fund for them. Nothing's made a dent. Meanwhile Lin and Troon are on uncertain ground with the Morngs. And their childhood is flying by in the blink of an eyelash. I don't plan to give up without a fight."

Removing his keys from the ignition, he got out and came around to hold the car door open for her. The tremor of excitement she felt when his hand brushed hers and the natural way they fell into step as they started toward the restaurant only confirmed her strong feeling that here was a man she could happily spend a lifetime with. Because of the accident she'd suffered as a teen, he could never be for her.

The pain of their situation hit her with renewed force as they took their places at a corner table. Aaron was so good to look at—lean, dark haired and handsome with the tawny eyes of a tiger. Not to mention decent. Funny and caring. Sharp as a tack. The way he'd kissed her left little doubt about what kind of lover he'd make.

How cruel fate was to dangle him in front of her, then snatch him away—almost in the same breath. It was as if a door had opened partway, only to slam shut in her face.

"Don't feel limited to a cheeseburger just because I mentioned one," he said, giving her a wry smile. "My budget can stand a steak."

"Actually, a cheeseburger sounds perfect tonight."

She could only pick at her excellent sandwich when it arrived. Aaron did a little better though he, too, seemed to have lost his appetite. Their conversation limped along in fits and starts. In answer to Aaron's questions, Kendra described her upbringing near Milwaukee, Wisconsin, as the only child of a dairy farmer and a former interior decorator. Shying away from too much emphasis on her parents' deaths in a boating accident on Lake Michigan shortly after her marriage to Glenn, she switched the topic to recent advances in cardiology.

We shouldn't be here at all, she told herself as she listened to him describe several new techniques. *Two weeks from now I'll be his student. Yet even if that weren't a factor, we could never have a serious relationship. I don't have the credentials to hope for permanency with him. And, though I may be old-fashioned, I'd never settle for an affair.*

After the waitress had removed their plates and he'd paid the bill, Aaron suggested they adjourn to the bar. While they'd been eating, a piano player had set up shop. A few couples were dancing now on the tiny parquet dance floor.

He ordered Scotch for himself and a dry martini for her. Perhaps by mutual consent, they barely sipped at their drinks, as if to draw out the evening to the last possible moment. For Kendra, the pleasure of Aaron's company was bittersweet. The jazzy, evocative music and amiable buzz of talk that filled the restaurant's crowded little bar area only served to heighten the sadness she felt.

Aaron knew he shouldn't ask her to dance. It would turn an innocent dinner together into something much more ill-advised. But he found it almost impossible to resist. After this evening, he guessed, they wouldn't be alone together. He wanted another chance to hold her, even if it had to be in a public place.

The way she was tapping her toe to the music hastened his decision. "C'mon," he said abruptly, pushing back his chair and holding out his hand. "Let's get it out of our system."

She almost said no. A reckless spirit wouldn't let her pass up the chance. You might as well indulge yourself while you can, it argued. Even if dancing with him will be a little like Daniel volunteering to enter the lions' den. Or a trapeze performer working without a net.

Getting to her feet, she came into his arms. Almost immediately the pianist, who was running long, coffee-colored fingers over the ivories behind the built-in piano bar, switched to an intimate, bluesy number. It spoke eloquently of love just out of reach.

At first Aaron held her almost formally, highly cognizant of the dangers that might lurk in a more familiar embrace. The sensual atmosphere, soft lights and their tantalizing proximity quickly undermined his resolve. With a sigh, he pulled her closer, so that his cheek rested against her hair.

Breathing in the mingled aroma of his after-shave and distinctive skin scent, she could feel the lean, hard muscles of his thighs moving against hers. Against all reason, longing blazed up, so willful and sweet it brought tears to her eyes. She couldn't keep from nestling against his chest.

My God, Aaron thought. The way she fills my arms! Though he'd been misguided to let it happen, he was more convinced than ever that he was falling in love with her.

Maybe he'd *always* loved her since he'd found her crying in the hospital parking lot.

For her sake he'd keep his feelings to himself. Yet they'd both pay a heavy price. As long as she remained his student, his conscience would bother him. And he'd be tougher on her than he was on the other residents to compensate. It wasn't fair, not by the furthest stretch of his imagination. But he didn't know how else to handle it.

Captured lovingly in his arms, Kendra didn't want the music to end. But she knew that, just by dancing together, they were risking their professional reputations. The whole idea of going out to dinner had been a mistake.

I've got to put a stop to this, she thought. Even if that means tripping over his feet. It was like a dash of cold water in her face when he withdrew first.

"Sorry to call a halt to such pleasant proceedings," he said casually, his gold-flecked eyes unreadable as he led her back to their table. "But I'm a little tired from my trip."

During the drive back to his house, neither of them said very much. This is it, Kendra told herself. The next time we see each other, we'll be professor and student with all the rigid mores that entails.

"Want to sit on the porch for a while and listen to the quiet?" Aaron asked as they pulled in to his driveway and parked beside her boxy little import.

In the process of steeling herself to say good-night to him, she gave him a startled look. "I thought you wanted to get to bed early."

On the dance floor at Ten Beach Drive, his urge to push too hard had been overwhelming. And he'd retreated the only way he could. Now that they were alone beneath a sky settling into night, he didn't want to let her go.

"Guess I just feel like talking," he said, not making any move to get out of the car.

Kendra's face was shadowed in the fading light. "Surely by now we're both talked out," she answered, remaining in her seat.

What would it be like, she wondered, if I'd come back to St. Petersburg with my residency finished, to work with him as an equal? What if I were capable of having his baby?

The thought of carrying Aaron's child inside her, of feeling it flutter and grow, made her heart ache. How wonderful it would have been to be able to give him a gift like that! she thought. Why, oh, why couldn't things have turned out that way?

Aaron was wishing with all his might that she'd selected another residency program—any program but his. He didn't want to evaluate her, criticize her, or get tough with her the way he always had to do with the budding specialists who were assigned to him. Instead, he wanted to hold her. Smooth her hair and tell her his innermost secrets. Make love to her every night.

The way she'd responded to his kiss in the airport parking garage had given him a taste of what a deepening relationship with her would be like. He wanted more, much more—anything and everything she had to give. Allowing his imagination free rein, he pictured himself leading her from the car and up to his bed, plundering the glory of her depths. But he wasn't sure that, if she chose to accompany him, they'd get past the stairs.

There are places on the grass, he thought wildly, places sheltered from prying eyes by a jungle of vegetation. We could take off our clothes and lie down together, let the dew caress our skin. Desire glowing in him like a red-hot poker, he imagined them taking each other to the brink of completion and moving past it until their longing was spent.

He was making love to her with his eyes! Overcome by the splendor of it, Kendra pictured his mouth crushing hers as if it were really happening. She could almost feel the delicious weight of his body.

With a start, she realized nothing had actually taken place. They hadn't moved. Or even touched. "I really should go," she said, freeing herself from the spell her thoughts had cast.

He gave himself a little shake. "When am I going to see you again?"

She glanced down, then met his eyes. "In about two weeks."

"At the resident staff meeting."

"Yes."

He regarded her silently for a moment. "You're right, of course. Anything else would put us both in an untenable position. And yet..."

The unfinished sentence hung between them fraught with possibilities. Kendra held her breath as, with a slight movement of his hand, he lifted a strand of her hair and let it go.

"I want to kiss you good night," he added. "For old times' sake. But I'm not going to do it."

She couldn't begin to tell him how much she regretted that. "Thanks for dinner, Aaron," she replied in a carefully controlled voice, getting out of the convertible. "See you at the hospital."

Driving back to Kim's house, Kendra marveled at how freely she'd responded to Aaron's touch. Like a violin to a master, she admitted to her sorrow. The only lover she'd known, Glenn had never made her feel so out of control, so powerless to refuse him. Never had he filled her with such tremulous expectation.

Yet she'd had no choice but to walk away. And he'd been right to let her go. It's going to be "Dr. Dash," not "Aaron," the next time we see each other, she thought. And I'll just have to live with that. If I get any ideas to the contrary, I have only to remember that even if it weren't for my residency I'd be barred from loving him.

Hoping to shift gears into neutral, she flopped down on the family-room couch and turned on a boring made-for-TV movie when she reached the Johanssens' house. The movie quickly degenerated and, picking up the remote control in disgust, Kendra punched the mute button. She shut her eyes.

Though she'd fantasized about Aaron for years, in her more rational moments she'd never expected him to make love to her. Tonight he'd wanted to. And she'd ached to let him. The fact that circumstances had forced them to back off only exacerbated her desire.

Damn, she thought, feeling the pain of it wash over her. I knew this year wasn't going to be easy. But I didn't expect it to be so difficult. From the vantage point of the Johanssens' couch on that cruel but lovely evening, she suspected the forthcoming trial of her endurance and moral fiber would be the toughest she'd ever had to face.

On Monday Kendra had lunch at the hospital cafeteria with her former boss, gray-haired, motherly Director of Nursing Bess Martin. Carrying their salads to an out-of-the-way table, they settled down for an in-depth chat.

"I'm very proud of you, dear child," Bess began, giving Kendra a fond look. "When you came to me that day and said you were quitting to study medicine, I wanted to jump for joy. Not because I was losing you as one of my head nurses. *That* was an inconvenience, to say the least. But I always felt you had what it took."

Kendra pretended to duck. "Thanks," she said, dimpling at the older woman's praise. "You're going to give me a swelled head."

"Nonsense." Bess speared half a cherry tomato and popped it into her mouth. "You know," she added after a moment, "not everyone has the guts to start over in life. I often wish I'd done it myself."

Touched by the nursing director's frank admission, Kendra shook her head. "I've got my M.D., but I'm not home free yet," she reminded her.

Bess laughed. "You're right...you picked a tough taskmaster in Aaron Dash. If I remember correctly, the two of you struck some rather eye-catching sparks on his first quarterly visit to SICU."

Alarmed at the turn their conversation was taking, Kendra didn't rise to the bait.

"By the way," Bess added, "I hear he's back in your life in more ways than one."

A frown drew Kendra's brows together at that. "I don't know what you mean."

"Oh, I think you do. A friend of a friend of mine saw the two of you doing some torchy dancing at Ten Beach Drive Saturday night. Pretty fast work, if you ask me. You've been back in town for less than a week."

So the rumors were flying about them already. She'd have to squelch them, and fast. Yet, try through she would, Kendra couldn't convince Bess there was nothing between her and the handsome cardiologist who'd be her professor of record. She was desperately attempting to change the subject when the first of two visitors stopped by their table. Abandoning her single-minded focus on Aaron at least for the moment, Bess introduced the impeccably dressed man with blue eyes and a receding hairline as Duane Calloway, the hospital's new administrator.

He gave Kendra an approving once-over. "Happy to meet you, Dr. Jenkins," he said. "Dr. Ames has told me so many good things about you. Just to set the record straight, I'm single. And partial to tall, good-looking redheads."

Their second visitor was Aaron. Speak of the devil, Kendra thought, squirming beneath Bess's amused I-told-you-so look. Unlike Duane, he made himself at home with his lunch tray. A study in healthy eating habits, it contained a tuna sandwich on whole wheat bread, yogurt, skim milk and an apple. His manner all business, he struck up a conversation with Bess about staffing problems.

Torn between feeling left out and gratitude that he hadn't embarrassed her by evincing too much interest, Kendra munched her lettuce and raw veggies in silence. It's clear he's heard the rumors, too, and decided to be circumspect, she thought. I should be grateful.

And of course she was.

Perversely, she wanted to feast on him with her eyes. In his white lab coat with a stethoscope sticking out of its breast pocket, he seemed remote, almost inaccessible. Yet he was as heart-stoppingly sexy as ever. On the verge of taking her lunch and moving to another table, Kendra couldn't think of a valid excuse.

Abruptly Bess got to her feet, explaining she had a 1:00 p.m. meeting in personnel. "I'd better be going, too," Kendra said quickly, picking up her tray.

"Hold on just a moment."

She half expected Aaron to catch her by the hand. But it wasn't really necessary. His will to keep her there was stronger than her urge to flee. Besides, he knew she wasn't on any kind of schedule yet. Surrendering, she sank back into her seat.

"The rumors about us are making the rounds already," he noted, his face expressionless.

She swallowed. "I'm aware of that."

"We can't give people any further reason to talk."

He was telling *her?* "Then why did you choose to sit with us?" she asked, a trifle irritated with him. "There must be at least three hundred hospital staffers in this cafeteria. And dozens of empty seats."

"People know we used to work together. Pretending otherwise will just fuel the fire."

"Okay," she conceded. "I'll go along with that. But must we overdo it? We've had our token conversation."

He regarded her steadily for a moment.

"Saturday night, during our dinner at Ten Beach Drive, you mentioned you'd never managed to locate the mother of your late husband's child. I thought you might want to ask the Morngs. It's possible they'd know something."

Self-conscious at the thought that people were probably staring at them, she drew a blank.

"They're the couple that brought Lin and Troon out of Thailand," he supplied. "I'm not sure if I mentioned it, but they run a restaurant on the south side called the Mango Tearoom. It's not very big and definitely not in a good neighborhood. But the chicken with *ngoc mam* and lime juice is excellent."

Kendra waited. There had to be more to it than that.

"If you'd like to talk to them," he continued, "I'd be happy to go along and translate."

It would be a chance to see him—and to give the rumors about them added credibility. "Thanks, but I don't think that would be a very good idea, considering your warning of a moment ago," she said, firmly gathering up her things. "If you'll excuse me, I have to run. I have another engagement this afternoon."

His manners exquisite as always, Aaron got to his feet. "Suit yourself," he said, keeping his voice low enough that he wouldn't be overheard. "You have only to let me know if you change your mind."

In fact, Kendra's only engagement was with the chaise longue on the Johanssens' patio. As she lay motionless on her stomach in a yellow bikini, covered from head to toe with a tanning preparation that promised to screen out the sun's harmful rays, she couldn't get Aaron out of her mind.

Cut-and-dried though it had been, her encounter with him in the hospital cafeteria had caused her renewed unhappiness. My feelings for him aren't going to go away, even if he starts dating someone else, she thought. But there's absolutely nothing I could do about it if he did.

Turning over on her back, she reached for the tall, insulated glass of lemonade at her elbow. Most of the ice in it had melted. Yet it was still cool enough to quench her thirst. If only heartaches were susceptible to such a simple remedy!

Making an effort to banish Aaron from her thoughts, she got only as far as the Morngs. It would have been interesting to see their place and the other child Aaron wants to adopt, she acknowledged. Even if they don't know anything about Song's whereabouts.

But perhaps they did.

Though she'd looked up Glenn's former mistress in the Tampa phone book on her first evening at Kim's house and subsequently tried Information, she hadn't turned up a clue. Meanwhile, it was common knowledge that refugees stuck together, forming networks of support in an alien environment. If the Morngs *did* know something, she might finally be able to put the issue of her responsibility to Glenn's child to rest. Surely they spoke a *little* English. How could they run a business otherwise?

By a quarter to five, Kendra was donning a pink halter jumpsuit and fastening gold hoops in her ears. Her mass of auburn hair lay like a bronze halo about her shoulders. I may as well dress up while I can, she thought wryly, surveying herself in the mirror. A week from now I'll be wearing a no-nonsense hairdo, sensible shoes and a white lab coat.

The Mango Tearoom wasn't difficult to locate. Jammed in between a barbecue stand and a pawnshop, it was modest indeed, though attempts had been made to give it an appealing air. A sign had been carefully lettered in English and Khmer script. Someone had hung lace curtains at the window.

During Kendra's drive south from the Johanssen residence, the afternoon thunderheads so typical of Florida in late August had grown increasingly threatening. Now, just as she got out of the car, the heavens opened. Rain came down in buckets. Having misplaced her umbrella, she dashed for the door with a newspaper over her head.

She'd forgotten Morng Ny was pregnant. In her cotton-print sarong, protruding blouse and sandals, the Cambodian woman appeared to be about five months along. Hurting as she pictured her late husband's lover carrying his baby, Kendra didn't respond when Ny clucked sympathetically over her rain-soaked state.

I should have known better than to come here, she thought, the old pain of her inability to have children assailing her. But how could she leave? It seemed she was the Morngs' only customer. She couldn't bear to disappoint

Ny, who smiled and bowed effusively as she led the way to a plastic-covered table.

Politely handing her a menu, Ny bowed again and disappeared in the direction of the kitchen. So far, not a word of English had been exchanged. I wonder if I'll be able to talk with the Morngs after all, Kendra thought. No wonder Aaron offered to translate.

Somehow she had to order, if only to fulfill Ny's pleased expectations. To her surprise, the tearoom's brief list of offerings was also lettered in both Khmer and English. Frowning, she began to study it. She jumped when a tall American sauntered out of the kitchen munching on a fried noodle confection.

"So you decided to come, after all," Aaron remarked nonchalantly as he sat down at her table.

"What . . . what are you doing here?" she croaked.

He gave her a sober look. "I have to eat."

It was impossible to argue with that.

"Besides," he added, turning the menu facedown as he prepared to order for them, "I happen to be an investor in the place. I come here several times a week. My partners can use the business."

Moments later Kendra found herself being formally introduced to Ny and her husband, Houm. The Cambodians appeared to regard her as Aaron's date. The misunderstanding made her feel awkward, to say the least. To her further chagrin, she couldn't seem to keep her gaze from resting on Ny's stomach.

It turned out that Houm was studying English in night school and he was eager to practice what he'd learned. With a great deal of help and some translation from Aaron, he explained that he, his wife and several other refugees ran the restaurant as a cooperative. He was one of the cooks. Ny took orders and waited on tables.

As he talked, Dith Lin, a charming, well-mannered child who'd picked up a smattering of English as well, came to stand by Aaron's chair. He's closer to the age Glenn's son or daughter would be than Troon, Kendra thought, pierced by a deep sadness. Yet she couldn't help warming to him, as she had to the older boy. The dinner she and Aaron shared in the little tearoom was both exotic and delicious. Kendra couldn't pronounce the names of the dishes that appeared, let alone guess at their contents. Yet to Aaron's obvious satisfaction, she declared herself impressed.

Watching him with Lin and the Morngs, she couldn't help but think how easily he fitted in with them. It was almost as if he felt *at home.* Maybe his determination to adopt Lin and Troon has something to do with military service in Indochina, she thought. I wonder if he fought there. And left a child behind.

She doubted if she'd dare to ask.

During their meal only one other diner, an elderly man, came into the restaurant. It was clear that, so far, Aaron's investment was yielding him few financial returns. Yet he was like a proud parent showing off a new baby, eager for compliments.

Houm returned to their table with the dessert and Kendra had a chance to ask him about Arn Song. Sadly, he'd never heard of her. But he promised to ask around.

It slipped out in conversation that Aaron spent a large percentage of his spare time and money operating a free clinic for the city's refugee population. "Thanks to Dr. Dash, many children get help when they sick," Houm said. "Mothers same. And fathers. We not know what we do without him."

The revelation only confirmed her feelings that Aaron's past was linked with Southeast Asians in some way, as well as her strong approval of his humanitarian bent.

Following repeated praise to Houm and Ny and more than a few wistful glances at Lin when she thought Aaron wasn't looking, Kendra accompanied him outside. It had stopped raining. The shabby neighborhood surrounding the restaurant was dripping in clean-washer.

Aaron laid one hand on her arm as she bid him good-night and started to get into her car. "I know we need to be careful about our conduct," he said. "But, strictly as a friend, I was wondering if you'd do me a favor. You mentioned your mother was a decorator and you probably learned a lot from her. Would you be willing to take a look at my house and tell me what it needs in the way of renovation and redecorating? I'd like to have several members of the refugee committee over when I finish, in hopes of changing their mind."

It was an intriguing prospect—one that would allow her to make a contribution to his planned adoption of Lin and Troon, however slight. Weighing the good she could do against the risk, Kendra decided to do as he asked.

"I suppose it would be all right," she said at last. "When would you like me to come over?"

The attractive grooves beside Aaron's mouth deepened just perceptibly. "How about tonight?"

Chapter Four

Calling herself every name in the book for what she considered her total lack of judgment, Kendra weakened. "Maybe for a few minutes," she said.

As she followed Aaron back to the house facing Coffee Pot Bayou, she was filled with mixed emotions.

While he remained single, the complex, special man who'd captured her heart probably wouldn't be allowed to adopt Lin and Troon. Married, he'd seek and get their custody in a minute. As his wife she'd be able to help him achieve that end. But even if it weren't for her residency, she'd never be able to marry him. She lacked a place inside her to grow the child he hoped to give a woman someday.

I don't know how I'm going to stand it, she thought. There doesn't seem to be an answer for us.

It wasn't dark, just early dusk as he let her in to the house. Light turned out to be at a premium in the living room. With an apology for the shadowy corners that might make decorating potential difficult to assess, he switched on a single floor lamp and some wall sconces that had seen better days.

Pushing aside any thought of regret, Kendra looked around in fascination. The floor, fashioned of narrow oak planks, had great possibilities. But it needed refinishing. She pictured it sanded, sealed and gleaming, framing a jewel-toned oriental rug. There wasn't enough furniture in the room to influence her vision of how it might look someday. A few pieces, grouped near the fireplace at one end, occupied perhaps a quarter of its space. She recognized most of them from her visit to his apartment six years before.

"I put my bookcases, stereo and the TV upstairs for the time being," Aaron explained.

Not answering, she headed into the dining room. Empty, it boasted a pair of lovely built-in oak cabinets with leaded-glass fronts. There was space for a buffet and a good-sized table. Unable to stop herself, Kendra imagined a family, *love* in the room. Faces flattered by the glow of candlelight. The tantalizing aromas of a holiday feast. Either you're crazy, she thought, or you enjoy tormenting yourself with visions of a future you can't share.

The kitchen had worn linoleum in a pattern that had been dreadful even when it was new. Its built-in cabinets had glass doors that matched those in the dining room. Originally painted white, the woodwork had yellowed to a soft ivory. Aaron's refrigerator and stove were relics. He had only one truly modern appliance to his name—a gleaming microwave oven.

His laundry area caused her to wince. Ditto the antiquated plumbing in the house's two and a half baths. The upstairs bedrooms, also floored in oak, were breezy and spacious. Just one, the largest, contained any furniture: his bed and dresser from the apartment plus the TV, stereo and bookcases he'd mentioned. It was the only room in the house that had a lived-in look.

"I don't spend much time downstairs except to throw an occasional meal together," he admitted, aware of what her impression must be.

In truth, to Kendra everything about the place *did* spell loneliness. His apartment had been comfortable, an appropriate haven for a single man to hang his hat and sometimes bring a woman. By moving into the house, he'd put himself in a completely different category. Now he was a family man without a family, rattling around in a place that was much too big for him. The very fact of his living here must make his desire to adopt Lin and Troon that much stronger, Kendra guessed.

"What you're facing here is an enormous job," she told him as they went back downstairs. "I could write a book about what this place needs."

"Pretty bad, huh?"

Ushering her into the kitchen, he retrieved two apples from the refrigerator and handed one to her. It was crispy cold.

"I wouldn't say that, exactly." Biting into the sweet Jonathan, she wiped a spurt of juice from her chin. "This place has lots of innate style and charm. It's just that nobody's done anything to it for years."

"That's it in a nutshell. What do you suggest?"

"Well, for starters..." Pausing, Kendra stared off into space as she mulled over a plan of attack.

Watching the wheels turn in her head, Aaron thought how good it was to have her under his roof. He had sisters—three of them, in fact—though they all lived out of state. He'd grown up with women around and he liked the way they thought. He truly admired the homey atmosphere they seemed so effortlessly to create. If Kendra and I were ever to live here as a couple, it wouldn't be all passion and fulfillment, he acknowledged, though we'd have plenty of that. There'd be quiet times, too. Cozy evenings by the fire.

Though Kendra had enjoyed scant opportunity to feather a nest during her nomadic military existence with Glenn and subsequently during her years in medical school, Aaron had been right on target: she *had* picked up a lot about decorating from her mother.

"Tell you what," she said, deciding to make him a present of her secondhand expertise. "I have a little time on my hands before I have to report to the hospital. If you'll leave your key under the mat, I'll look around for some samples and model numbers, come back and make up a list of what you need. Fair enough?"

Aaron grinned at her, delighted. "I'd say it's more than fair."

"Then you have a deal." She'd make a point of stopping by while he was at work.

A workaholic for most of her adult life, Kendra dove with gusto into the task she'd set for herself. In addition to benefiting Aaron, she hoped her efforts would distract her from too many melancholy thoughts.

Early the next morning she was running around town in her little car, stopping here and there to talk with plumbers, appliance and flooring dealers, painting and refinishing contractors. She even checked out several furniture stores and a few ads for used items she'd circled in the classified. In the process, she collected a stack of brochures and quite a few samples. By Wednesday afternoon she was ready to look at them in the context of the house.

As promised, Aaron had left her a key. Fitting it into the lock, she had the oddest feeling of coming home. Easy does it, she cautioned herself. This is nothing more than a favor you're doing for a friend. Make that a favor for your about-to-be boss. But she knew Aaron's status at the hospital had little to do with the energy and caring she'd poured into the project to date.

Clad in a rose pink halter that bared her midriff, and abbreviated white denim shorts, she was standing in the kitchen, thoughtfully weighing wallpaper swatches against paint chips and several varieties of tile samples when she heard a footstep behind her. Startled, she almost jumped out of her skin. It was Aaron.

"What are you doing here?" she demanded accusingly. "I thought you'd be at the hospital for quite a while yet."

A muscle twitched beside his mouth. "I live here, remember? And this is my afternoon off. We had a light schedule at the clinic, so..."

She didn't answer. Her lips were moist and softly parted, almost too tempting to resist. Somehow he managed it.

"Do I dare mention how nice it is to come home and find you here?" he asked, standing so close that his breath mingled with hers. "Or should I just ask to see the samples you've collected?"

The simple fact of his nearness was enough to make her forget every pledge she'd ever made to herself. But her residency was now just twelve days away. All too soon she'd be facing him across the chasm that separated professor and student.

"Maybe you'd better ask to see the samples," she decided, stepping out of reach.

He didn't argue. Getting out two chilled cans of soda, he transferred a pizza from freezer to oven and set a portable timer.

"Okay," he said. "Let's see what you've got."

It didn't escape her notice that the pizza was big enough for two. While it heated, they spread Kendra's booty out on the countertop, arranging and rearranging things until they'd come up with several possible combinations.

"You didn't say anything about cost," she noted. "And I know a good deal of your salary and fees go into the clinic. So I came up with some options on the big-ticket items. They range all the way from budget to sky's the limit. I'd recommend a middle-of-the-road approach."

Aaron wanted to give her an approving hug. Not only was she sexy, dedicated and brainy as hell if her grades were any indication, the title M.D. after her name with its money-making potential hadn't turned her head.

"As it happens, middle of the road is exactly what I had in mind," he assured her as the timer rang. "Excuse me a moment while I get our pizza out of the oven."

Carrying the food and the rest of Kendra's haul out on the porch, they settled comfortably on the glider with the pizza resting between them on its cardboard carton. Almost too hot to eat and somewhat on the gooey side, the pizza tended to get all over everything. They were forced to lick their fingers repeatedly as they went over brochures on plumbing and electric light fixtures and her suggestions for refinishing the floors and woodwork. For some reason, the casual sloppiness of the meal lulled her misgivings that they were edging back toward dangerous ground.

"Once the basics are done," Kendra noted as she picked off a slice of pepperoni and popped it into her mouth, "you'll want to shop for furniture."

Aaron polished off his second piece. "Any chance I can count on some additional help?"

"That depends on you. As my resident professor, you'll be able to lay claim to my every waking moment."

She'd intended it as a joke. Somehow the words had come out wrong, suggesting a lien on her person wholly different from the one she'd had in mind.

"What about the sleeping ones?" he teased. "Did you intend to issue a *blanket* statement?"

Though his response was obviously intended as a pun, Aaron's eyes had taken on their smoky look. Kendra felt as if she were rooted to the spot.

"You know what I meant," she whispered.

As they gazed at each other over the remains of their supper and the brochures she'd brought, desire was an almost tangible thing. If they stuck to the rules, they couldn't do anything to satisfy it. With difficulty Kendra kept tears of frustration from welling up in her eyes.

Aaron watched the play of emotions on her face.

"Hey," he growled, sweeping the pizza leftovers to the floor and wrapping his arms around her, "don't cry, Redhead. I'm sorry if my teasing upset you. It's just that I want you so damn much. And I don't know what to do about it...."

It felt wonderful just to rest her cheek on his shoulder. "Neither do I," she admitted, the words scarcely above a breath.

A thousand thoughts were competing in Aaron's head. Uppermost was the achingly sweet realization that she wanted him, too. Maybe if he spoke to Bert Ames, juggled the schedule around...

Yet what possible reason could he give the resident director that wouldn't cause problems for Kendra or earn him a severe reprimand? He could hardly explain he'd thought of her on and off for years and, now that she was back within reach, he wanted to make love to her.

Though it was the literal truth, he'd begun to want a lot more than that. He just couldn't say so. They needed time—the chance to know each other better and allow their relationship to develop some depth and breadth. He wished professional ethics hadn't precluded that, just as he wished he could sit on his back porch and share a pizza with her without wanting to take her to bed.

"I ought to go," Kendra said softly, her eyes shut and her palms resting against his chest.

"And I ought to see you to the door. But..."

It struck him that, once the resident year began, the gap between them would widen. Instinctively he pulled her closer in his arms.

A moment later she was succumbing to the temporary insanity of his kiss. Gently at first, with infinite tenderness, he took possession of her mouth. Need opened to meet him. Just as it had in the airport parking garage, the citadel of her separateness flung open its gates.

With the speed of sound, of light, their passion escalated. Her breath caught in her throat as he reached inside her halter top to caress her breasts. Yes... oh, yes! she exulted at the arousal of her sensitive peaks. You're what I've wanted...what I've *needed.* I've been wild to have you touch me this way.

Somehow—she wasn't quite sure how it happened—she found herself all but sitting on his lap. The ties of her halter top had come undone and it fell forward, spilling out her lush fullness into his hands. The glider rocked as he deepened his kiss until it became a foretaste of the act of love itself.

All but drowned out by the tumult of Kendra's emotions, the voice of reason struggled to be heard. *No,* it pleaded harshly. You're making a big mistake. Even if you don't give a damn about your residency, you can't belong to him.

With a little moan at what it cost her, she pushed him away. "Aaron, please!" she begged, hastily covering herself as she got to her feet. "We can't do this...."

The glider swung back abruptly as he followed suit. Her cheeks were flushed, her bright hair disarranged in a tangled halo about her face as she looked up at him. With all the ardor he possessed, he wanted to love her senseless, please her thoroughly. But he knew the most loving thing he could do for her would be to refrain from touching her again.

"You're right," he conceded, his firmly chiseled features taut with self-recrimination. "God knows I've behaved like a jackass. I won't ask you to forgive me this time...just to believe it won't happen again."

"It...wasn't all your fault."

"That's a matter of opinion."

His voice was so hard, so uncompromising it hurt to listen. With every tender emotion she possessed, she longed to comfort him. "I suppose," she faltered after a moment, "that I'd better go...."

He nodded his agreement. "I really think you should."

Though it went against the grain, he didn't see her out. He planned to keep his promise. And that meant avoiding any and all "occasions of sin." From the porch, he listened as the light rhythm of her footsteps crossed the bare floor of the living room and the front door closed softly behind her. Moments later her car started. There was a spurt of gravel as she backed out of the driveway.

A hint of her perfume lingered on the air. It made Aaron want to throw things. There was only one cure for the way he felt and that was exercise. His expression grim enough to terrorize the most confident nurse or phlegmatic resident, he went upstairs and changed into his running clothes.

Kendra's heart was like lead when she picked up Kim and Dan on Friday at the airport. By contrast, her friends were bubbling over, full of stories about their godchild and plans to have a baby of their own. Kim announced that she hoped to go off the pill as soon as she could talk with her gynecologist.

Pleased as she was at her friends' happiness, it only threw Kendra's misery into sharper relief. She couldn't have the man she loved and she couldn't have a baby. I need a place of my own, she thought. Somewhere I can crash after a killing day at the hospital and pretend there's no such thing as being in love.

Ignoring the Johanssens' protests that she was welcome to stay as long as she liked, she rented an apartment the following day and moved in that afternoon. A furnished efficiency in a down-at-the-heels, semitransient neighborhood near the hospital, it reflected her state of mind. One more year in the tunnel, she promised herself, and you'll be free to live and work wherever you choose. One thing was certain. It would be far, far away from the handsome, dark-haired cardiologist who made her yearn for might-have-beens.

The phone company installed her new line on Wednesday and somehow Aaron got hold of the number. "Hi," he said awkwardly. "I thought you might like to know...the downstairs painting's going great. And the refinishers are scheduled to begin work on Monday. Because you were able to get the ball rolling, this place has a fairly good chance of turning into a real home."

With effort she chased the longing from her voice. "I'm glad to hear it," she acknowledged. "You're a fast worker."

This time he didn't pounce on her unintended pun with one of his own. "Well, I just wanted to thank you," he said after a slight pause. "I really do appreciate what you did."

"I was happy to help."

Damn, thought Aaron. I shouldn't have called. We're like Alphonse and Gaston, the two legendary Frenchmen exchanging pleasantries while they try to decide who should go through a doorway first. But there was something else he'd wanted to tell her.

"When we were at the Mango Tearoom last week," he said, "you commented you'd like to see the clinic before your residency starts. You'd be more than welcome. I mentioned you to Lucy Ong, my assistant, in case it's more convenient for you to drop by while I'm at the hospital. She'll be glad to show you around."

Fascinated by anything even remotely connected with Aaron, Kendra drove over to the converted residence that housed the St. Petersburg Free Clinic for Southeast Asians early the following afternoon, choosing a time when she knew he'd be occupied with surgery or postsurgical rounds. On Thursdays, he'd told her, the clinic didn't open its doors until 1:00 p.m. Lucy covered until Aaron was free to help.

There weren't many patients in the waiting room—just a few mothers with babies or young children who needed shots or something for a cough. But according to Aaron it could get hectic. He'd recruited Lucy, a middle-aged nurse and registered physician's assistant of Chinese ancestry who'd been born in Cambodia. She possessed the skills to work with youngsters and old people and she knew several Southeast Asian languages.

"Very nice to meet you, Dr. Jenkins." The thickset, motherly woman beamed. "Dr. Dash told me you'd be visiting us. Please...come this way."

As they took a quick tour of the well-equipped treatment rooms and color-coded records areas, Lucy made no effort to hide her strong admiration and loyalty for her boss. If she felt any curiosity about Kendra's relationship with him she kept it to herself.

"As his friend," Lucy said emphatically, "I'm sure you'll agree—a busy specialist who donates his free time to help struggling refugees is something rare and wonderful. My husband and I think the world of him."

As she drove away, Kendra had to concur with Lucy's statement. I wish I could help out with what they're doing, she thought. I'd offer if I wasn't afraid it might be a conflict of interest. She knew that if it weren't for her inability to have children she'd be daydreaming that she and Aaron could marry and operate the clinic together once her residency was completed. She couldn't imagine a greater happiness.

At the initial resident staff meeting, Kendra and Aaron met as strangers. She hadn't phoned him after visiting the clinic. And he hadn't called again. Apparently the invitation to check out his pet project had been a kind of added apology or a subtle attempt to get their relationship back on a strictly medicine-related footing.

One of several dozen new residents, she sat in the second row, anonymous in a white lab coat with her mane of auburn hair pulled back into an uncompromising bun. The wire-rimmed glasses perched on her nose gave her a businesslike air.

Dr. Ames made a few introductory remarks. Behind him, Aaron, Dr. Pete Bradley, the orthopod, Dr. Maureen Hamilton, the oncologist, and several physicians she didn't know waited quietly to meet with their individual residents. His dark brows drawn together, Aaron swept the new crop of faces with a hard, professional gaze. She couldn't detect a flicker of recognition in his eyes.

His impersonal manner didn't change when she and the other four cardiology candidates met with him to discuss routines and responsibilities.

"You'll each have at least three patients assigned to you as your particular charge at any given time," he said crisply. "Sometimes as many as half a dozen. I expect you to look after them as if you were the only doctor on the case."

Reaching into his briefcase, he passed out a roster of current patient assignments. Kendra was disappointed when Sem Troon's name wasn't listed beneath her own. Before she could speculate about why Aaron had chosen to assign the boy to someone else, they were off and running, making rounds, visiting patients and checking out the quarters they'd use when they were on overnight call.

By exercising iron control, she kept the memory of what had almost happened between them from interfering with her work. But it was a definite struggle. Each rapier-sharp glance from his hazel eyes threatened to undermine her resolve. *I hope to God this gets easier with time,* she thought. *Because if it doesn't, I don't know what I'm going to do with myself.*

As she headed into the fifth week of her residency, Kendra's relationship with Aaron was as cut-and-dried as any program director could wish. If anything, he appeared to be tougher on her than he was on his other residents. He also seemed a shade more distant.

Her head swimming with new surgical techniques, complex patient charts and heavy responsibilities, she still missed their budding closeness. The coldly formal interaction that had taken its place was a very poor substitute, though it gave her no cause for complaint from an ethical standpoint.

Seeing him every day, accompanying him on rounds and closely assisting him in surgery wasn't easy. Yet perhaps because she was focused on her work and prepared for those moments, they weren't among the worst she had to face. The really difficult times arose when she wasn't thinking about him at all. To her chagrin, off-duty encounters or glimpses of him at a distance seemed to hurt the most.

One afternoon he settled at a table next to hers in the cafeteria and plunged into an animated conversation with several nurses. She was close to the breaking point. Look, she told herself, even if you could find a way around the restrictions imposed by your residency, nothing's changed. You still can't be part of his future. The result is kismet. Fate.

Then she and a fellow resident, good-looking, affable Tom Bennett, were called on to assist Aaron in an operation to correct the life-threatening heart abnormalities of a newborn infant. It was a tricky case and the child nearly died on the table. At one point Tom panicked and for several minutes Kendra and Aaron had to handle the crisis without his help.

Though it was touch and go, they managed to pull the baby through. Finally all the sutures were in place. At Aaron's nod, a surgical aide transported the infant to the recovery room.

"He's going to make it, isn't he?" Kendra asked.

"So it would appear."

The terse comment stung until she realized his displeasure wasn't with her. Clearly hoping to postpone Aaron's censure, Tom had thrown off his mask the moment they were finished and hightailed it out of the surgical suite.

Touched by the sensitivity he displayed, Kendra watched and listened as Aaron gave a brief report to the baby's parents. A few minutes later they were standing side by side at the scrub-room sinks. Out of the blue he gave her the first compliment she'd received in more than a month of straining to do her best.

"You did a damn fine job in there," he grumbled, glancing briefly in her direction.

"Thanks. I appreciate it."

More undone by a kind word than any brusqueness he could have employed, Kendra had a distinct lump in her throat. In the operating room they'd been a team, thinking, anticipating and acting like one person. Now the distance was back, despite his grudging approval. And it hurt.

Switching off the tap and turning away from the sink, she bumped directly into him. Are there magnets, she wondered, that pull us together the moment we let down our guard?

Whatever the case, it was déjà vu. Aaron steadied her with his hands on her shoulders. Yet for all the similarity to their meeting on the airport concourse, a lot had changed. For one thing, the strands of their lives had become more tightly interwoven. For another, denial had taken its toll.

Drilling into hers, for once his tawny eyes didn't hide what he felt. "Rough, isn't it?" he asked as if the fate of civilization hung on her reply.

She wasn't quite sure if he meant the responsibility they'd shared for a tiny, precious scrap of humanity or their mutual attempts to stay clear of each other. Either way, her answer had to be yes.

"You bet your sweet life it is," she said.

With the force of a tidal wave, he pulled her against his body. Seconds later they were kissing—hungrily, desperately, as if to devour each other there in the scrub room with its easy access to the hall.

It was a busy hospital and inevitably someone started to walk in. There was a slight cough as Dr. Marani, one of the plastic surgeons, beat a hasty retreat.

"That tears it," Aaron said, abruptly releasing her. "Marani's a compulsive tattletale."

Still blazing from his kiss, Kendra couldn't face another guilty, anguished postmortem over their bad judgment. Murmuring something inane and barely comprehensible, she darted from the room. He didn't follow. It was her half day off and, after another peek into the recovery room with instructions to the nurses where to reach her if an emergency arose involving her small patient, she fled. She was long gone, parked down by the harbor watching storm clouds pile up over the water, by the time Aaron was ready to leave the hospital.

He was headed for the stairs when Dr. Ames asked to speak with him in his office. Damn, thought Aaron. Here it comes. Marani has tattled, as expected.

"Is it true," Bert Ames said without preamble the moment his door was shut, "that you made improper advances to one of the female residents in the scrub room this afternoon?"

Ever one to face the music unflinchingly when that was called for, Aaron nodded. "Let me say up front that what happened wasn't Dr. Jenkins's fault. I take full responsibility."

The program director waved him to a chair. "I don't like having to get tough with you over something like this," he said, taking off his glasses and polishing them before returning them to his nose. "You're one of our finest specialists and teachers. And until now, your record at this hospital has been without blemish. But, damn it, Aaron.... We can't have that kind of thing going on!"

Well aware he'd made a serious blunder, Aaron didn't try to gloss things over. He didn't present an argument in his own defense. Instead, "I was wrong, Bert," he acknowledged promptly. "I apologize."

Dr. Ames's expression softened a little. "Fraternizing with the residents could undermine everything we're trying to achieve, as I'm sure you realize," he said. "No doubt what happened this afternoon resulted from stress. God knows, an operation like the Brown baby's takes its toll on everyone. And even in surgical scrubs, Kendra's an eyeful...."

Aaron had to agree with the resident director's assessment of her.

"I suppose you know there's been gossip—stemming, it's true, from the weeks before her residency started, but gossip nonetheless," Dr. Ames continued. "This incident will only lend it credence, I'm afraid. I trust nothing of the sort will happen again."

The line of Aaron's jaw was like granite. "I promise," he said. "No more indiscretions in the scrub room." He only hoped he'd be able to keep his word.

Chapter Five

That night Kendra got very little sleep. Tossing and turning in her narrow bed, she went over and over the scrub-room incident. She felt branded by Aaron's kiss—and its heart-stopping aftermath. What would have happened if Dr. Marani hadn't come in? she wondered, punching her pillow into a different shape. Would the barriers between us have fallen? Or would they have remained in place, more insurmountable than ever? She guessed it would have been the latter. Aaron was as concerned about ethics as she was. And, though he didn't realize it, ethical considerations weren't the only thing keeping them apart.

Whatever the case, Dr. Marani *had* come in. And they'd found themselves facing a whole new set of complications. She asked herself miserably if the whole thing was her fault. She hadn't initiated the kiss. But she'd responded to it. Oh, how she'd responded. Like a desert traveler offered a chance to slake her thirst! Maybe if I could manage to look where I'm going and stop bumping into him, she thought, we might have a prayer of avoiding each other.

Unfortunately the damage was already done. At that very moment rumors about what had transpired between them were probably spreading in ever-widening circles. She knew gossip could sweep a self-contained community like the hospital in minutes; she'd seen it happen. It could make working conditions intolerable and destroy careers.

She'd be lucky if Dr. Ames didn't put her on probation or boot her out of the program. And, though he was in a loftier position than her, Aaron might find himself in trouble, too. If Dr. Marani chose to create a big enough fuss, he could be hauled in front of the joint medical school-hospital board. Or even suspended.

Before the ramifications of their indiscretion were fully known, they'd have to face the other residents. It wouldn't be easy for Aaron. But at least he was in a position of authority. Kendra feared her partners on the cardiology team would think she was attempting to sleep her way to a good evaluation. If they only knew, she thought. Nothing could be further from the truth.

For her, the most difficult thing of all would be facing Aaron himself. She felt guilty, regretful—and yet charged as if by an electrical current with the knowledge that he wanted her. Wrong though she'd known it to be, during the delirious seconds she'd spent in his arms, relief had almost surpassed her desperate feeling of need for him. However briefly, overcoming the emotional distance that separated them had given her a profound sense of being where she belonged.

The following day at the hospital a few snide remarks were made within her hearing, but nothing she couldn't handle. None of them came from people she'd begun to consider friends. As for Aaron, his mask of stern professionalism was firmly back in place. In a way she was grateful. She managed to get through the day by concentrating on patient welfare while thoroughly ignoring her own.

She ran into Duane Calloway late that afternoon when she was walking to her car. "Hi, how's Children's treating you?" the sandy-haired administrator inquired with a smile.

He hasn't heard, Kendra thought. Or I'd get a nod at best. Then again, maybe he's the sort of person who doesn't let idle talk make up his mind for him.

"No complaints," she said, starting to move past him. "Have a nice evening."

To her surprise, Duane fell in step with her. He's going to ask me about it, she thought, overcome with a sudden feeling of panic. How on earth am I going to respond to him?

It turned out that Duane had something totally different in mind. "I'd like you to be my date for the medical staff banquet next week if you don't already have a previous engagement," he said, throwing her for a loop. "I've already checked your overnight schedule and you have the evening off."

Despite his comments in the cafeteria a month earlier about being partial to redheads, Kendra hadn't thought of Duane Calloway as a potential date—probably because she couldn't see anyone but Aaron in that light. She tried to wipe the astonishment off her face.

"Say something," the affable administrator joked. "Attending the banquet with me can't be that awful to contemplate. Or are you staring at me like that because I've managed to get red ink on my forehead? I've been working on the budget this afternoon!"

"No, of course it isn't," Kendra stammered. "And you haven't. It's just that I—I'm so involved right now in my work."

"Everybody needs to relax occasionally."

It struck her that Duane was unwittingly offering a chance to squelch the gossip about her and Aaron. As the hospital administrator, he was in charge of Children's regular employees. But he was only indirectly connected with its residency program. Though he sometimes attended meetings of the joint hospital-university board that oversaw the program, he did so only as an observer, not a member. He had nothing to do with resident evaluations.

If she went to the banquet as his date, people would start talking about them instead. But there wouldn't be any suggestion of a conflict of interest. She just wasn't sure it would be fair to use Duane that way.

"I don't know..." she began uncertainly.

"Look," he interposed. "For all I know, you're interested in someone else. If so, that's okay. My invitation still stands. The woman I've been seeing on and off for several years backed out on me at the last minute and you're my first choice to be her replacement. I'd be honored if you'd accept."

When you put it like that, Kendra told him silently, I can hardly refuse. She didn't stop to think that Aaron might be planning to attend the banquet, too. Or worry about the kind of impression he might get.

"Thanks, Duane. I'd love to go with you," she said.

The week preceding the event didn't turn out to be an easy one. For one thing, Kendra's schedule was especially wearing. One of her fellow residents got sick and she had to take up part of the slack. For another, she couldn't get the scene with Aaron in the scrub room out of her head.

He hadn't apologized this time, perhaps feeling as she did that enough I'm-sorrys had been said. His demeanor as they worked together didn't offer a clue about his inner feelings. He seemed determined to prove there was nothing between them by being tougher on her than before. Pointedly criticizing the way she'd handled one of her absent colleague's patients and making much of what she knew were nonexistent flaws in her performance, he had the other residents assigned to him shaking their heads.

I have all the drawbacks of a love relationship with him, she thought—sleepless nights, a more exacting standard to meet than anyone else and the knowledge that, even though I'll be seen in public with Duane, the gossip about us will probably die a lingering death.

Yet I'm deprived of all the benefits. Getting too specific about those, she knew, would be an exercise in brinkmanship that could all too easily slip out of control.

Absorbed in her thoughts as she walked from her car to the hospital the morning of the banquet, she didn't notice the straggly, undernourished white kitten until it rubbed against her ankles.

"Poor little thing," she sympathized, stopping to pet it. "You're probably lost."

Its bones prominent beneath matted fur, the kitten began to purr with the smooth, steady sound of a well-oiled engine. "You're just like Lin and Troon," she told the kitten, wondering if Aaron had made any headway with the refugee association. "You probably need a home."

When she passed that way again, going in the opposite direction at the end of her half-day shift, the kitten was still hanging around. On impulse she scooped it up.

"C'mon, Tofu," she said, calling it by the first name that came into her head. "I know a place that isn't very fancy. But there's milk in the refrigerator. And the lady of the house is willing to spring for some cat food. The only price you'll have to pay is a bath to get rid of those terrible fleas."

After a stop at the grocery store, she headed home to bathe Tofu in the kitchen sink. Though he obviously considered water and soapsuds an affront to his pint-sized dignity, the kitten endured them without squirming or clawing at her hands. He was actually purring by the time she was seated on the couch, drying him in a fluffy towel.

The landlord will probably have a fit if he finds out I've adopted an animal, she thought, setting out a dish of soft food and a bowl of milk. Yet as she watched the grateful kitten chow down on his serving of liver and chicken, then lap up the cold, fresh milk, she was determined to keep him.

"We'll just have to convince Mr. Fossi what a model pet you are," she murmured, smoothing the fur over his knobby little backbone.

Getting ready for the banquet brought Kendra's misgivings back to the fore. By now it had occurred to her that Aaron might attend and she dreaded coming face-to-face with him as she entered the yacht club on Duane's arm. As she bathed, dried herself and slipped into a black silk gown with narrow shoulder straps that she'd bought for the occasion, she tried to imagine what her dark-haired supervisor would think if he saw her with Duane. Something told her he wouldn't like it very much. But she couldn't see how attending the function with the hospital administrator could drive them any further apart.

Spraying on her favorite perfume in front of the bathroom mirror, she realized it was probably a mistake to let her hair tumble in riotous abandon about her shoulders.

Few of her colleagues from Children's Memorial had seen her that way. Unbound, the mass of coppery curls gave her an almost wanton look.

She decided not to put it up in a chignon despite her reservations. She couldn't have Aaron—not now, not ever. Yet a perverse spirit in her wanted him to yearn after what might have been, the way she did. As the doorbell rang, she acknowledged that same renegade self was probably hoping for a miracle to take place.

Duane let out a wolf whistle when she opened the door. "What happened to cool, professional Dr. Jenkins?" he demanded, obviously impressed. "In that dress, you look like a movie star."

As she and Duane drove up to the yacht club entrance, Dr. Ames happened to be talking with several of his colleagues and their wives on the front steps. He'd been out of town for several days. Kendra hadn't spoken with him since the scrub-room incident. She couldn't suppress her satisfaction at his look of surprise.

It went without saying he'd never have expected her to arrive with Aaron. Yet, thanks to Dr. Marani's likely tale carrying, the chances were better than ever he saw the two of them as emotionally involved. He appeared to be rapidly rethinking that idea, now that she'd come as Duane's date.

Approval radiated in his smile. "Good evening, Kendra, Duane," he said in his courtly fashion as they turned Duane's sedan over to the parking attendant. "You're looking lovely tonight, young lady. I'd like you to meet my wife, Betty. Dear, this is Dr. Kendra Jenkins, who used to be our head nurse on Surgical Intensive Care. You know Duane, of course. Kendra's come back to us for her residency and she's doing an outstanding job."

As luck would have it, they were seated at the Ames's table. Glancing surreptitiously around, Kendra didn't see Aaron. Maybe the annual staff banquet is too stuffy for his taste, she thought, praying he wouldn't show.

She'd begun to relax a little when he walked in—late, alone and lithe as a jaguar in his perfectly tailored evening clothes. Spotting her, he paused in the act of pulling out a chair at the table where his fellow residency professors, Dr. Hamilton and Dr. Bradley, and their mates were seated. Kendra winced at the astonishment on his face. She wanted to hide from his carefully controlled displeasure at seeing her with another man.

She hadn't really wanted the martini Duane had ordered for her. Now she found herself needing something to bolster her resolve. Turning away so that neither Aaron nor anyone else in the room would guess how much she wished they could have come together, she downed a healthy swig of gin and vermouth.

"Tell me, Duane," she said, her voice too brittle, her eyes too bright. "Do you have to give a speech tonight? If so, I don't envy you. I've loathed public speaking ever since I was in high school."

By some quirk of fate, Aaron turned up next to her in the buffet line. Betty Ames separated her from Duane.

"Good evening, Dr. Dash," she said with as much nonchalance as she could muster. She knew it would only create more talk if they didn't speak.

"Dr. Jenkins." A muscle quirked beside his mouth. "I wasn't aware you and Duane Calloway were such good friends."

"We're not." The words were out before she could stop them. But she'd spoken softly. She didn't think either Betty or Duane had overheard. "I mean . . . we've only known each other a short time," she amended, lowering her voice still further. "As I'm sure you recall, Duane didn't work at Children's six years ago."

"There's no need to explain."

His expression forbidding, Aaron speared several jumbo shrimp for his plate.

Loving him though she did, Kendra felt her temper rise. He isn't making a difficult situation any easier, she thought irritably, dipping into the crabmeat salad. I don't like this any better than he does. Preoccupied, she lifted a spoonful of salad toward her plate. To her horror it banged into the buffet's Plexiglas hood. Crabmeat, celery and mayonnaise skidded into a vat of cocktail sauce.

The faux pas attracted Betty Ames's attention. "Tut, tut, my dear," teased the resident director's wife, her pleasant, motherly face creasing in a smile. "You'll never make it as a heart surgeon if you can't handle the most basic implements!"

Her cheeks flaming, Kendra tossed a mishmash of items onto her plate and beat a hasty retreat. Good grief, she thought, surveying her spur-of-the-moment choices and trying to appear unruffled for Duane's sake. I don't even *like* herring in sour cream. Half this stuff is going to go to waste.

Doing her best to hold up her end of the conversation, Kendra barely tasted her meal. At last the dessert plates had been removed and the obligatory speeches by medical staff officers were history. A musical combo started to play.

Seemingly unaware that she was having a dreadful time, Duane asked her to dance. Though he was very nice and he'd done everything possible to make her feel appreciated, pretending to enjoy herself as she moved to the music in his arms was almost beyond Kendra's capacity for theater.

With a determined effort she managed to keep from glancing too often in Aaron's direction. But she knew he wasn't having much fun, either. Frequently alone as his colleagues danced with their mates, he nursed a watered-down Scotch and stared morosely off into space. No doubt it was obvious to all and sundry that he'd have preferred to be anywhere else on the globe.

She wondered why he didn't just go. *I* would if I didn't have to consider Duane's feelings, she thought. As it is, I'll probably have to see this out to the bitter end.

Just then Duane's beeper went off. The administrator made a wry face. "I knew it was too good to be true—a whole evening without urgent phone calls and my usual responsibilities," he said, walking her back to their table and excusing himself to phone the hospital.

Duane's features were arranged in a rueful expression when he returned to the banquet room. The Ameses and the Mossmans, the other doctor and his wife who'd shared their table, were dancing. Like Aaron, Kendra was alone.

"I'm doubly sorry because it's going to spoil the rest of our evening," the administrator told Kendra, leaning over her chair. "But a severe child-abuse case has turned up in the emergency room. Since we're currently between public information directors, I'll have to handle it myself. I doubt if I'll be able to make it back here before the party's over."

"Oh, no. I'm sorry, too." Kendra started to get up, assuming she'd accompany him.

The administrator forestalled her with one hand on her shoulder. "You needn't leave simply because I must," he said. "I don't have time to take you home first and you'd only get stuck at the hospital...probably for hours. As I'm well aware, you spend quite a bit of time there already. The most sensible thing you could do would be to stay and enjoy the party. I'll leave you cab fare in case Bert and Betty Ames can't give you a lift."

Kendra glanced at the program director and his spouse, who were dancing at the opposite end of the room. "I'm sure they wouldn't mind," she began. "But really, Duane... I'd be only too happy to..."

Her escort didn't seem to guess she'd give anything to walk out of the yacht club and put the evening behind her—even if that meant waiting at the hospital until his crisis was resolved. If worse came to worst, she could take a cab home from there.

"It's truly not necessary," Duane insisted, betraying some impatience. Before she could stop him, he was slipping her a ten-spot. "I'll touch base with you in the morning, all right?"

A few minutes later Kendra was forced to explain her escort's absence to Bert and Betty Ames. "Duane thought you might be able to run me home," she murmured, reluctant to impose on them.

Husband and wife looked at each other in distress. "Oh, my dear!" Betty exclaimed with genuine regret. "There's nothing we'd like better. But I'm afraid we won't be able to unless you feel like making a round trip to the airport first. Our son, who attends college in Michigan, is bringing his fiancée home for a visit. We have to pick them up in Tampa this evening. We were just about to say our goodbyes to everyone. I'm sure Ken and Silvia Mossman would be glad to help."

The last thing Kendra wanted to do was intrude on a family situation. Or take advantage of Dr. Mossman and his wife. She didn't know either of them very well.

Luckily the Mossmans were still on the dance floor. "I'm sure you're right," she replied. "Don't give it another thought. If you'll excuse me, I need to make a quick visit to the powder room."

She was standing by the pay phone in the bar, dialing for a taxi, when Aaron came up behind her. "Where's your date?" he asked.

Kendra jumped at the rough-lush texture of his voice. Temporarily abandoning her call, she turned to face him. "A really bad child-abuse case came in," she said, striving for a poised, detached air. "Apparently there'll be some publicity. Duane felt he ought to handle it himself. The Ameses had to pick up their son and his fiancée in Tampa. So..."

"You're calling a cab."

She nodded.

He stood there looking down at her for a moment, as if considering a range of possibilities. "No doubt it will unleash the furies of hell," he said at last, "but I'll take you. I was leaving, anyway. C'mon, let's go."

He didn't give her a chance to protest. As if they were racewalking or straining to meet an imminent deadline, he ushered her swiftly out of the yacht club and down the steps.

"I'm not much for valet parking," he said curtly, taking her arm. "My car is several blocks away."

Keeping up with him despite her high heels, Kendra hurried at Aaron's side along the quay with its rows of sleek, expensive sailboats. In her mind's eye, every passing car contained someone from the hospital who couldn't wait to spread the word that they were fraternizing again.

Gradually Aaron's pace slackened. The breeze was soft, the evening like velvet. Halyards struck the forest of aluminum masts with a sound like temple bells. With the Mustang in sight a hundred yards or so down the street, they paused beside a thirty-foot sloop fitted with blue sail covers.

"What do you say we go aboard?" Aaron asked, his beautiful eyes unreadable. "I haven't wanted to approach you at the hospital. But we really ought to talk."

Kendra felt an unreasoning tug of fear. Was he going to ask her to resign? Or transfer her to another professor? The Aaron she knew would hardly do either. And he was the only cardiologist who worked with residents. . . .

"I suppose it would be all right," she said tentatively, "provided the owner wouldn't object."

"I have it on good authority he wouldn't." Straddling the gap between seawall and boat, Aaron pulled the mooring line taut and offered her his hand. Removing her shoes so they wouldn't damage the decking, she stepped aboard.

So, she thought, trying to pull herself together. The boat is his. God knows hc deserves a little relaxation. Absolutely nobody works harder than he does.

"What's her name?" she asked in a small voice.

Giving her an enigmatic look, he pulled out a pair of canvas cushions. "Didn't you notice? It's *The One Who Got Away.*"

Something about his expression made her heart beat faster even as it quelled her fears. She considered his answer as she took a seat. The name sounded as if it referred to a prize catch that had slipped off his line in the past. But how odd for him to personify a fish.

"I didn't realize you were an avid fisherman," she said.

"The name has nothing to do with that."

For several minutes they sat in silence, gazing out over the harbor. There were lights on some of the boats, bleeding copper and golden into the inky water. The relaxed, peaceful sounds of people spending a quiet evening aboard

This lovely Victorian pewter-finish miniature is perfect for displaying a treasured photograph—and it's yours absolutely free—when you accept our no-risk offer.

DETACH AND MAIL CARD TODAY

PLAY "LUCKY 7"

Just scratch off the silver box with a coin.
Then check below to see which gifts you get.

YES! I have scratched off the silver box. Please send me all the gifts for which I qualify. I understand I am under no obligation to purchase any books, as explained on the opposite page.

215 CIS ADEQ
(U-SIL-R-10/91)

NAME

ADDRESS APT.

CITY STATE ZIP

7	7	7	WORTH FOUR FREE BOOKS, FREE VICTORIAN PICTURE FRAME AND MYSTERY BONUS
cherry	cherry	cherry	WORTH FOUR FREE BOOKS AND MYSTERY BONUS
plum	plum	plum	WORTH FOUR FREE BOOKS
bell	bell	cherry	WORTH TWO FREE BOOKS

Offer limited to one per household and not valid to current Silhouette Romance™ subscribers. All orders subject to approval.

PRINTED IN U.S.A.

SILHOUETTE "NO RISK" GUARANTEE

- You're not required to buy a single book—ever!
- You must be completely satisfied or you may cancel at any time simply by sending us a note or a shipping statement marked "cancel" or by returning any shipment to us at our cost. Either way, you will receive no more books; you'll have no obligation to buy.
- The free books and gifts you receive from this "Lucky 7" offer remain yours to keep no matter what you decide.

If offer card is missing, write to:
Silhouette Reader Service, 3010 Walden Ave., P.O. Box 1867, Buffalo, N.Y. 14269-1867

DETACH AND MAIL CARD TODAY

BUSINESS REPLY MAIL
FIRST CLASS MAIL PERMIT NO. 717 BUFFALO, NY

POSTAGE WILL BE PAID BY ADDRESSEE

SILHOUETTE READER SERVICE
3010 WALDEN AVE
PO BOX 1867
BUFFALO NY 14240-9952

NO POSTAGE
NECESSARY
IF MAILED
IN THE
UNITED STATES

their craft carried to them in snatches through the balmy air.

A few clouds that looked as if they might contain some rain had come up from the west. We shouldn't do this, Kendra thought, enjoying the freshening breeze on her face and the sloop's gentle rocking motion. We're just asking for trouble. Yet there was nowhere else she'd rather be. The opportunity to spend time with Aaron away from the hospital was such an unexpected bonus she wanted to pinch herself.

She was about to conclude he'd changed his mind about talking when he spoke her name—just the single word.

"Yes?" she whispered.

"The boat isn't mine. It belongs to Pete Bradley and his wife, Joan. I don't have enough free time to make ownership practical. They let me use her once in a while."

Too bad, she thought. This man, so conscious of his healing gift, gives too much of himself. He needs a little pleasure in his life. The chance to relax more. A woman and children to love. In addition to Lin and Troon, he needs his own children—something I can never give him.

"Her name is *Halcyon Daze,*" he added.

"Then why did you tell me—"

"Because if she *were* my boat, I'd name her after you."

A light sheen of goose bumps covered Kendra's bare arms. Six years earlier she'd left without saying goodbye to him. Now, though he'd told her how pleased he was that she'd earned her medical degree, he was implying the selfish man in him hadn't wanted her to go.

With the chiaroscuro quality of heat lightning, the series of intimate encounters they'd shared since her return to St. Petersburg flickered through her mind. From their first kiss at the airport—slow, sweet and abruptly so passionate she'd wanted to offer him her soul—to their fierce embrace in the scrub room, the closeness that seemed somehow to have developed during their years apart had deepened. She wanted him so much now she thought her heart would break.

"What happened last Thursday in the scrub room can never be repeated," he said, choosing that moment to speak his mind. "I'm sure you know that as well as I do. I'd also like you to realize I regard the incident as entirely my fault."

Stubbornly Kendra shook her head. "I don't agree."

His tawny eyes searched her face. "If that's true, you must be feeling some of the tension and frustration I do. It's begun to interfere with my work. . . ."

It seemed she'd been right all along. "Do you want me to resign?" she asked, trembling.

A heartfelt oath escaped him. "Have you lost your mind? You're one of the best things that's happened to that program in a long time. If you quit, so do I."

"You don't mean that."

"Try me."

They stared at each other for a moment, neither of them willing to give an inch.

"Damn ethical responsibilities, Kendra!" he said in exasperation, the lush corduroy texture of his voice very pronounced. "Haven't you guessed that every harsh, impersonal word I speak to you feels like hell to me? I'm walking around that hospital with my gut hanging out, aching to make love to you!"

Chapter Six

It was what she wanted, too. The thought of connecting so profoundly with Aaron's power and hunger made her want to forget everything that stood in the way—professional ethics, the fact that she couldn't give him a baby, even her own deeply ingrained conviction that sex outside of marriage cheapened what a man and woman could share.

In the long run he could never be for her. If she wanted to taste the splendor of his lovemaking, she'd have to settle for a furtive banquet, a single night of mind-drugging pleasure in a lifetime of loneliness.

"Maybe I do know it," she confessed, her words blurring with need. "Maybe I want you, too."

Just then the breeze quickened. A few raindrops began to fall.

"Your dress," Aaron murmured, stripping off his jacket and settling it over her shoulders. "It's going to pour."

Already the light patter of the rain had quickened. They'd be soaked if they tried to run for the car. Digging in the pocket of his trousers, Aaron produced his keys and fitted one into the cabin lock.

"Pete gave it to me," he explained as they ducked inside.

There wasn't much space in the combined galley and sleeping area. They found themselves half in each other's arms. But they couldn't change their minds about seeking shelter. Big, squally raindrops had begun to pepper the sloop's fiberglass, metal and wood surfaces.

"You were saying?" Aaron asked quietly, resting his hands on her shoulders.

Kendra bit her lip. Succumbing to temptation now with barely six weeks of her residency completed would be nothing short of a disaster. They'd never be able to go on working together.

Yet something in her that was deeply oblivious to practicality wanted him to know how she felt. Her voice was a whisper. "Maybe I want you, too."

The reluctant admission was all it took to push him past the brink. With a groan he pulled her into his arms. His mouth took complete possession of hers. Worshipfully he ran his hands over the silk-smoothed contours of her body.

Their need for each other had been building for years. To satisfy it, if only for a few stolen moments, was like being released from a kind of prison. Kendra didn't object when he swept her dress's spaghetti straps down her arms and molded the lower half of her body more intimately against his.

How long they kissed that way she couldn't have said afterward. In one way it had seemed like forever. In another, that moment carved out of time was lived in accelerated motion—tumbling them, hurtling them to a point of no return.

For Kendra, just letting him hold her was like manna to a starving person. He smelled of soap and sunlight, after-shave blended with the scent of his freshly laundered evening shirt. Even so, the clean, never-to-be-forgotten aroma of his skin was the dominant note. She wanted to drink it into her pores.

What she wanted most was Aaron, claiming the hidden privacy of her womanhood. The sensations aroused by his hands as he caressed her breasts through the thin fabric of her silk gown knifed her to the quick. It was as if an instant telegraph connected her erect buds to her most erotic self.

With Glenn she'd never achieved fulfillment and somehow she'd never expected to. She knew making love with Aaron would be different. She imagined him filling her, drawing her up a fiery ascent. Craving more from him, more, she'd arch her body away from the sloop's narrow bunk to meet him. Fulfillment would soar beyond the bounds of their physical selves.

Once joined so profoundly, she guessed, there'd be no turning back for them. Yet she couldn't give Aaron what he'd told her he wanted—his own child someday.

No, she thought. You can't do this. It wouldn't be fair to him.

"Ah, sweetheart," he muttered, not yet aware of the anguish she felt. "I've wanted you for so long...."

It was too late. Willingly she'd have waited for him until her residency was over, willingly married him and helped him adopt two orphan boys. But she was barred from a life with him by a handicap he knew nothing about. A sob catching in her throat, she turned away.

Aaron's hands stilled. "What's wrong?"

"What we're doing isn't right."

To her consternation, he didn't release her. Instead he rested his cheek against her hair. "Tonight, when I asked you to sit on the boat and talk," he said, "I was planning to tell you the same thing. I never had any intention of making love to you."

"Then..."

"What I *planned* to say was that I couldn't stand for us to be at odds anymore. And that your residency won't last forever. I hoped we could come to some kind of understanding. Next year there won't be any ethical considerations in the way. I'd like to court you...."

She didn't say a word.

"Please, Redhead," he begged. "You're not making this any easier. Say that's what you want me to do."

It was what she wanted more than anything in the world. But she couldn't allow it to happen. Once her residency was over, she'd be forced to put as much distance as possible between herself and the man she loved.

"I could never let you do that, Aaron," she said.

He did let go of her then. "Mind telling me why not?" he asked, the words bereft of all expression.

"It...would never work."

His silence demanded more. It wasn't forthcoming.

"Is it that you don't trust men because of what your late husband did?" he asked in frustration, his temper escalating a notch. "I can't believe that...any more than I can believe you don't feel something for me that's slightly more profound than lust. Give me a reason, damn it! I want to know!"

The truth was on the tip of her tongue. She was about to confess everything when a little voice whispered he'd say it didn't matter—even if it mattered the earth.

He raked his fingers through his hair when she didn't do as he asked. "It's Lin and Troon, isn't it?" he demanded, grasping at straws. "You're afraid if you committed to me you'd get stuck with them!"

The pain in her eyes told him his accusation was wide off the mark. What the hell do you think you're doing? he asked himself, suddenly ashamed. You have no right to rake her over the coals this way. She doesn't owe you an explanation.

"Look," he said after a long pause, his voice going crisp and impersonal. "The rain has almost stopped. If you'll wait here, I'll run and get the car."

A few moments later he was pulling up at the curb. Back in medical school, if anyone had told me I'd turn down Aaron Dash, I'd have insisted they were crazy, she thought as he helped her off the boat and into the Mustang's passenger seat. Now I don't seem to have any other choice.

They didn't talk on the way to her apartment.

"This is it, then," he said as they halted in front of the converted house where she lived.

"Yes. I guess it is."

She looked so unhappy, so bereft he almost reached for her. But he realized that if she didn't want to tell him what the problem was there was nothing he could do about it. As he hesitated, Kendra got out of the car.

"Good night, Aaron," she said. "Thanks for the ride. See you at the hospital."

They were curt and impersonal with each other during morning rounds. The presence of shadows beneath Kendra's eyes testified to her lack of sleep. So did Aaron's irritability. Dragging despite her best efforts, she wasn't sure if she'd be able to make it through the day.

The only bright spot on her horizon was the Brown baby's marked improvement after a week on the critical list. She and Aaron were able to share a moment of satisfaction about that despite the wall that was firmly back in place between them.

Though a few stories circulated about Duane being called away from the banquet and Aaron taking her home, they died out almost immediately thanks to their standoffish behavior toward each other. To Kendra's knowledge, Dr. Ames didn't call Aaron into his office. The warning she herself expected to get from the resident director never came.

Settling down to a routine, she tried to lose herself in her work. She spent long hours at the hospital over and above her grueling schedule. Similarly dedicated, Aaron resumed his highly critical scrutiny of her performance. As if for good measure, he tightened the screws on the other residents, as well.

She refused to let the unresolved issues between them affect her work. Yet the heartache that gnawed at her insides and the way she insisted on driving herself took their toll. Finally Kim mentioned she was losing weight. And Bess Martin asked point-blank what the trouble was.

Kendra was having a hurried cup of coffee in the nursing director's office when Bess posed the question.

"Nothing's wrong," she insisted, trying to cover up her distress.

Characteristically, Bess dug deeper. "Nonsense," she replied in her brisk way. "If I'm not mistaken, your problem is about six feet two inches tall and has eyes like smoky topaz lasers. If you weren't so bogged down in your own view of things, you'd see that he's as miserable as you are."

"Do you really think he is?" Instead of experiencing regret, Kendra felt energized by the news.

"Indeed I do," answered Bess with a smile. "Can you honestly say that whatever's making you both so unhappy is worth the pain?"

Longing to tell Bess her secret, Kendra hesitated.

"You won't always have to answer to him for grades and references," the older woman added after a moment. "And his behavior won't always have to be above reproach. If your reasons for shunning each other go deeper than that, maybe you'd better reexamine them."

The nursing director's forthright words rang in Kendra's ears at lunchtime when she overheard Aaron and Pete Bradley discussing Troon's case.

"His leg is healing nicely. I plan to take the cast off tomorrow," Pete was saying.

Aaron nodded. "Then it's time to do the pacemaker. If he tolerates that well, we'll do the valve within a month."

Just then, Kendra's page sounded. Interested in the boy's case because of Aaron's affection for him, she was forced to leave the cafeteria on the run, thus missing out on the rest of their conversation.

Glancing at her, Pete shook his head. "You probably won't thank me for pointing this out," he told Aaron, "but you haven't been yourself lately."

Aaron gave him a wry look. "I take it I've been too easygoing, too cooperative."

Pete grinned. "In a pig's eye. But at least you can joke about it. Since we've traded medical services over the years, I don't feel as if I'd be out of place by offering a diagnosis. You're in love, old man. And your condition isn't going to get any better if you persist in shutting the lady in question out of your life."

There wasn't any doubt that Pete was referring to Kendra. Did the whole world know how he felt about her, for God's sake?

"Shut her out, hell!" he growled. "What do you expect me to do? I'm her residency professor. She's off-limits."

"It's not as if the situation is going to last forever.'

His feelings about Kendra were so private that Aaron was reluctant to share them with his friend. But he'd never felt more wretched in his life. He needed Pete's advice.

"Don't you think I know that?" he countered. "The night of the banquet, I talked to her about it. I even admitted I'd like to court her when her residency is over. She turned me down flat."

Pete shrugged. "So you're giving up on the first try," he said. "How persistent of you. I chased after Joan for months before she finally agreed to marry me."

Kendra was alone the following afternoon, dictating a report in the physicians' transcript room when Aaron walked in. She switched off her microphone immediately. "Anything wrong with Joshua Franklin?" she asked, naming the four-year-old they'd operated on that morning. "I looked in on him less than half an hour ago."

"No...Josh is fine." Aaron took a seat beside her at the long table with its row of dictation equipment. "I've got to talk to you."

No, please, she thought. Not again. But of course this time it wouldn't be personal. Instead she'd made some terrible mistake or been remiss with one of her patients. Her nerves on edge, Kendra waited for him to speak.

He fixed her with his honey-colored gaze. "I've got one hell of a temper and the night we talked on the Bradleys' boat I let it get the best of me," he said. "I want you to know my intentions haven't changed despite any reservations you might have. When your residency's finished, I'd like to court you. In the meantime, there's no reason for us to behave like strangers, or what's worse, enemies. We might even think about becoming friends."

Having expected a reprimand, Kendra was stunned. Though in reality it was a fishbowl, the glassed-in transcription room suddenly felt like a very private place.

"At least think about it," Aaron added, his demeanor casual enough to satisfy even the most skeptical observer that their conversation was all business. "If I'm not mistaken, the rift between us has been difficult for us both."

Her green eyes bored into his hazel ones from behind the wire-rimmed glasses she wore at work. "You're right about that," she admitted in a small voice.

"Then you agree?" He'd vowed he would get some kind of commitment from her.

What could she say? That she didn't want to be friends with him? Telling him that would be a lie. Meanwhile, though limiting their relationship might prove difficult, at least she wouldn't be starved for the sight of him, or aching for the sound of his voice. Instead of sparring, they could laugh once in a while. Maybe even touch, if only by accident.

"Okay," she said. "Friends it is."

His mouth curved in a smile that was like sunlight after rain. "Good," he answered. "I consider that progress. Maybe whatever you didn't feel like telling me on the boat will resolve itself."

I wish I could believe that, she thought, feasting her eyes on his firmly chiseled features and broad shoulders. *But there are some things not even determination and love can change.*

Seconds later he was squeezing her hand and walking briskly out of the room. *I hope what we're contemplating isn't a mistake*, she added to herself. *The last thing I want to do is mislead him.* As she rested her chin on her hand, the patient update she'd been dictating was a million light-years from her head.

Several days later in the cafeteria, Aaron told her about the installation of Troon's pacemaker. "The whole procedure went beautifully," he said. "The lead wires into the heart were some of the easiest I've ever done."

"I'm glad," Kendra answered. "He's a gallant boy. He deserves to live a normal, healthy life."

Following their brief talk in the transcription room, they'd begun to have coffee together. And though Aaron continued to be exacting when it came to professional matters, there hadn't been any more scathing lectures or unreasonable demands. He'd actually eased up on the other residents.

With some of the tension between them defused, she found herself getting to know him in unexpected ways. Half the time he's a health nut, wolfing down tuna, cottage cheese and fruit on the run, she thought fondly. The other half, he exists on junk food. Today he's in his junk food phase.

As he bit into a chocolate-glazed doughnut, she reran a conversation she'd overheard him have that morning with Jeff Carpentier, one of Pete Bradley's residents. Jeff had expressed an interest in volunteering at the Southeast Asian clinic. Jeff explained he'd had a free ride through school, on scholarship. "I'd like to give something back," he said. "Helping the Southeast Asian refugees will give me a chance to do that."

Aaron had accepted the offer. And Kendra had mulled it over during morning rounds. Maybe I could volunteer, too, she thought now. I won't be able to once my residency is finished if I leave the area. This may be my only chance.

"What would you say if I told you I'd like to help out at the clinic like Jeff?" she asked abruptly. "Do you think that would be all right?"

Aaron wiped a few doughnut crumbs from the corners of his mouth. "I think it would be fine," he answered. "It's not as if you'd be the only one volunteering from the program."

They edged closer as the days passed, cautiously testing the parameters they'd set for themselves. Simultaneously their professional rapport grew. Yet for Kendra their emotional truce was bittersweet. She wished with all her heart it could lead to what Aaron apparently envisioned—the chance to think about life together when their student-professor relationship was over.

Drawn like a moth to a flame at the prospect of what that life could be like, she began stopping by to see Troon, though he wasn't her patient. On one occasion she brought him some animal hand puppets she'd noticed in a toy-shop window.

Troon's dark eyes widened at the gift. "Tahk-you, Doctor Jen-kun!" he exclaimed, stumbling over a language that still largely eluded him.

He laughed out loud when she inserted her hand into a fierce-looking tiger and pretended to swoop down at his face. Unlike some other puppets she'd seen that represented the human characters of Western fairy tales, the brightly colored animals cut across cultural and ethnic boundaries. For the first time she and Troon were able to communicate. They managed to have an actual conversation—he in Khmer and she in English—via growls, squeaks and exaggerated gestures.

"Looks like the two of you are having a great time," Aaron remarked, poking his head in the door.

But he didn't stay long. They'd agreed on limits and he was going to abide by them. Still, as he walked off down the hall it did his heart good to know two people he cared deeply about were getting to know and like each other.

Kendra began volunteering at the clinic on Wednesday afternoons. During her fourth visit there, Lucy remarked that the following Wednesday was Aaron's birthday. He'd left his wallet lying open on his desk a few weeks earlier and she'd read the date on his driver's license.

"He's not the sort of man you buy balloons and a birthday cake for," Lucy added when the two of them were alone for a moment.

"No, he isn't," Kendra agreed. "Can you think of something else he might like instead?"

Lucy's face lit in a pleased smile at Kendra's willingness to be a coconspirator. "I know," she said. "Dr. Dash loves Ted Peters's smoked fish. Maybe we could take him out for a late lunch next week after office hours."

When they broached their proposal to Aaron, he couldn't hide his surprise. But he readily agreed that he'd be delighted to be their guest. The following Wednesday they had a light patient load. They were just finishing up when Lucy got a phone call from her husband, a retired computer expert. As she listened, a worried frown creased her forehead.

"Robert says our daughter Li, who lives in Cocoa Beach, just arrived with her new baby and every suitcase she owns," the physician's assistant reported in a strained voice when she put down the receiver. "Apparently she's had a fight with her husband. Robert isn't good with things like that. I have to go home and handle it."

"That's okay," Aaron told her. "We'll manage."

"But I don't want to ruin your birthday party, Dr. Dash!" Her anxiety plain, Lucy shifted her gaze to Kendra. "You take him, okay, Dr. Jenkins?" she asked. "Next week we'll split the bill."

"Maybe we shouldn't go, now that it's just the two of us," Kendra ventured after Lucy had gathered up her things and hurried out the door.

Aaron was silent a moment. "You're telling me I should celebrate my birthday alone? What would Lucy say?"

She'd be very disappointed in me, Kendra thought. And I'd have to agree with her. "When you put it like that..."

"You'll go."

"Yes."

"Good." Holding the door for her, he paused to lock up behind them. "I don't see how the powers-that-be could object if two friends eat smoked fish in front of God and everybody," he added. "Even Bert Ames wouldn't have a problem with that."

They drove out Corey Causeway with the top down, awash in a breeze-bath of air. As they ate at one of the funky little eatery's scarred picnic tables and toasted Aaron's birthday with soft drinks in paper cups, Kendra could feel something perilously close to contentment sinking into her bones.

Each day the bond between us gets a little deeper, she acknowledged. Is it possible he could change his mind about wanting to father a child someday? Would I even dare ask?

Tossing their paper plates into the waste bin when they finished, they got back into the car. "What do you say we head out to the beach for a walk?" he proposed. "It's my birthday, after all. Afterward, I'll drive you back to town."

She hesitated. "Okay."

They pulled out into traffic. On impulse she switched on the radio, adjusting it to a station that played mostly jazz. Almost immediately the music was interrupted by a news bulletin.

"This just in," the announcer said in a shocked voice. "According to police, a concrete truck lost its brakes just moments ago on St. Petersburg's busy Thirty-Fourth Street, careened down a railroad overpass and plowed into a school bus. The bus was reportedly stopped for a red light at Thirty-Eighth Avenue North.

"Police say it was carrying forty-two children—all of them Vietnamese and other Southeast Asian refugees returning from special after-school classes in English as a second language. Early reports indicate a number of fatalities have occurred...."

Kendra and Aaron looked at each other in horror.

"Dith Lin," she croaked, barely able to put the fear that gripped her into words. "Troon's little friend. Could he possibly have been on that bus?"

Chapter Seven

Aaron didn't answer right away. He made a screaming U-turn, narrowly missing a city bus and several other vehicles. A cacophony of horns sounded. Furious, the driver of a pickup truck shot them an obscene gesture.

His expression grim, Aaron didn't seem to notice. The indicator on the Mustang's speedometer jumped as, leaning heavily on the gas pedal, he concentrated on getting them back to town. "In answer to your question," he said in a voice she barely recognized, "Lin *has* been attending those classes."

"Oh, no!"

Shivering despite the mild autumn temperature, Kendra was overcome with a feeling of dread. The attractive, almond-eyed child who'd smiled at her so shyly during her visit to the Morngs' restaurant *couldn't* be lying on the pavement, hurt and bleeding. Or worse.

Aaron had the same picture in his head. Dear God, please don't let this be happening, he prayed, gripping the

Mustang's steering wheel. Lin's life is just beginning. All he's ever known is tragedy and separation. Let him live. Let him be all right. Please... Give me a chance to adopt him and make a home for him.

Seconds later he was praying shamefacedly for the other children, too. Lin was ineffably dear, a child he wanted to make his own. But the other youthful passengers on the bus deserved a crack at life, too. Some of them had probably been his patients at the clinic. Most of them mattered to someone. If they didn't—if they were essentially without anyone who truly cared for them, like the ragged waifs who'd saved his life in Vietnam—well, that was a separate injustice. At the moment he couldn't deal with it. But he *could* do his damnedest to improve their odds.

Kendra thought she was going to throw up when they reached the scene. As a physician and former nurse who'd worked with quite a few accident victims in her career, she'd seen some pretty horrible things. None of them compared with the grotesque sight of a concrete mixer accordioned into a bright yellow school bus. The dizzying arcs of light thrown off by a squadron of police cars and ambulances seemed only to accentuate the nausea she felt.

Parking on the grassy verge of the partially blocked-off street behind a police cruiser, Aaron snatched up the emergency medical bag he kept under the driver's seat. "C'mon," he said roughly, getting out of the car. "We don't have a moment to lose."

Kendra followed, her distress at the spectacle they faced growing at a geometric rate. A police officer with a harried expression barred their approach.

"We're doctors," Aaron snapped impatiently.

"Okay," the cop answered, giving way. "We can use the help."

Somehow she got hold of herself. They ran forward, crunching over broken glass and splashing through puddles that had been created when a fire truck had hosed down the impacted vehicles.

Up close, the unthinkable tableau of the accident was even more gruesome to behold. There were so many wounded children! Several lay in unnatural positions, ominously still. Others cried out in pain and fear. Thus far, only the worst cases were being treated by overworked paramedics.

If Lin *had* been on the bus, there wasn't any sign of him. They didn't have time to make a thorough search. Terribly wounded children in plain view demanded their immediate attention. Maybe he played hooky this afternoon to help Houm and Ny, Aaron told himself, hoping against hope. Maybe he stayed home with a head cold.

Tight-lipped and dry-eyed, they pitched in to the triage work that had to be done before any of the small accident victims could be moved. There's absolutely nothing fair about this, Kendra thought. These children have already been through so much.

With so many youngsters in need of help, it was difficult to determine which ones required immediate transport to a hospital and which could afford to wait. Obviously grateful to be let off the hook when it came to the decision making, the hard-pressed paramedics deferred to them. Kendra realized that the choices they were forced to make in the blink of an eyelash could affect life and death.

More ambulances kept arriving as she and Aaron worked frantically to stem the bleeding from deep cuts, splint some of the worst compound fractures she'd ever seen and test for concussion and internal injuries. Soon the medical helicopter that served the Children's Memorial-

Bayport hospital complex landed in the intersection, ready to begin ferrying the most critical patients. They didn't see Lin anywhere.

At first Aaron had feared Kendra might pass out from the carnage they faced. If she had, he wouldn't have been able to stop and help her. Now, as she worked beside him, her hands were steady, her brain a marvel of efficiency. He could tell she had her emotions under solid control.

It was called grace under pressure. "You're good... damn good," he praised her shortly as they secured a small Vietnamese girl with head injuries on a stretcher.

"Thanks," she responded, wishing her ability to deal with a crisis wasn't being tested that way. "I'm only glad I was with you this afternoon."

"I'm *damn* glad you turned on the radio."

Just then one of the paramedics came running over to them. "Doc," he panted, addressing Aaron, "there's one left on the bus. Could you please come and have a look? I'm not sure we ought to move him."

A shudder that presaged emptiness and a future laid waste went through her. Her stockings torn by sandburs and bloodstains on her skirt, she stumbled after Aaron. Together they mounted the steps of the wrecked vehicle, fear stopping their breath.

For a moment they didn't see him. Then their gaze fastened on a small foot in a battered tennis shoe poking out from beneath one of the jumbled seats. It was Lin. Ashen and still, Troon's best friend lay like a rag doll amid the scattered and bloodied possessions of his classmates. "Dear God," Kendra breathed. "Don't let this be happening. Don't let him die."

Though a muscle tightened in Aaron's jaw, he didn't hesitate. Gently but urgently he bent over the twisted form of the boy he wanted to make his son. Undeterred by the cramped space, he took Lin's pulse and listened for his heartbeat as Kendra gripped the seat handles in suspense.

"He's still alive," Aaron muttered, testing the odd angle of Lin's neck with exquisite care. "Pulse faint and somewhat erratic. Spine, head and chest injuries, probably critical. We can't operate on him here."

Thanks to her medical training, Kendra could guess what he was leaving unsaid. If they tried to move Lin and made the slightest error, he might be paralyzed for life—that is, if they could save him.

Yet she agreed that moving Lin was his only chance. Stepping over the debris that blocked the aisle while Aaron was still examining him, she yelled for the helicopter paramedics to bring a stretcher.

"You'll have to handle him like nitroglycerin," she advised when they came running. "Better radio ahead for Josh Reidy. He's going to need the best."

Aaron glanced up at her. There was such pain in his eyes that she longed to comfort him.

"Asking for Josh was a good idea," he said, confirming her assessment that a topflight neurosurgeon would be needed. "Make sure they bring a backboard."

As the paramedics lifted Lin with extreme caution, strapped him in and rushed him toward the helicopter, one of the staff physicians from Bayport whose route north had taken him past the accident scene stopped to help. Spotting him, Aaron came to a quick decision.

"Dan Rosenberg's here," he said, hurriedly tossing Kendra his car keys. "I'm going with Lin in the chopper. Stay and do what you can."

"Okay." Turning away, she bent over yet another small patient.

For more than an hour Kendra remained at the accident scene, toiling beside the unfamiliar physician and an ever-changing battery of paramedics. Almost but not quite, her trance of efficiency let her ignore the deep anguish that kept welling up in her chest at the thought of what might be happening at the hospital.

Gradually they made their way to the least injured victims, applying nonstick bandages instead of tourniquets, splints instead of backboards. She took a deep breath as the last ambulance pulled away, its siren flailing at the air. Already the evidence of what had transpired was being erased. Wreckers were towing away the concrete mixer and the school bus. A city road crew had arrived to sweep up twisted metal and broken glass.

The policeman who'd detained them on their arrival was attempting to get the afternoon's hopelessly snarled rush-hour traffic moving again as she walked back to the car. He paused to shake their hand.

"Fine job, miss. I mean *doc,*" he complimented her.

Kendra wiped some of the grit and perspiration from her face. "Thanks," she said. "Any idea how many children were killed?"

The cop added up the known fatalities in his head. "Three, maybe four here at the scene," he said. "Probably a couple more at the hospital. I don't give that little tyke who was still on the bus much of a chance."

Abruptly, precipitously, she was furious enough to wring his neck. "I hope to God you're wrong!" she snapped, getting into the Mustang and turning Aaron's key in the ignition.

The policeman's expression didn't change. With a calmer part of herself, she knew what had happened wasn't the officer's fault. No doubt he'd seen a lot of accidents, too many injured and dying people. Though it clearly didn't please him, he appeared to stand by his conviction as he held up a long line of impatient motorists so she could depart.

The policeman with his dire prediction was out of mind before he was out of sight. Now that she'd finished her task at the accident scene, Kendra had only one thought in her head—to get to the hospital as quickly as possible. Breaking so many traffic laws that she lost count, she managed to reach the Children's Memorial parking lot in eight minutes flat without being stopped by the police.

She didn't bother to comb her hair or check her dirt-streaked countenance in the rearview mirror before hurling herself into the lobby. One of the doctors she knew stopped to ask her if there was anything he could do. Brushing off his well-meaning inquiry with a shake of her head, she chose not to wait for an elevator. Instead, she raced up the stairs to the teaching gallery, hoping to find Lin in the adjoining surgical suite.

It was where they'd taken him. Bert Ames and several other members of the teaching staff were already there, observing as Josh Reidy, assisted by Aaron and Pete, labored to pull Lin back from the brink.

"Kendra!" Dr. Ames exclaimed. "My dear young lady, what's happened to you? You look as if you've been through a knockdown, drag-out fight!"

Despite what Aaron had said earlier, Kendra knew Dr. Ames wouldn't be pleased to learn that they'd been out together. At the moment, what he thought—and whether or not they were guilty of any wrongdoing—didn't seem to matter a hoot.

"I was with Aaron at the accident scene," she admitted, allowing him to draw whatever conclusion he wished. Her mind and heart half-paralyzed with fear, sorrow and a thousand misgivings, she focused her attention on the huddled surgeons and nurses who were struggling to save Lin's life.

The operation was clearly touch and go. With such severe injuries, the slight, golden-skinned boy on the table was already in extreme peril. When his condition took a turn for the worse, the strain of that shift began to tell on the faces that surrounded him.

From her position at the gallery window, Kendra couldn't make out the subtle variations in the rows of jagged green lines that represented Lin's heartbeat and other vital signs on the monitor. But even from her vantage point she could see they were terribly erratic. Every instinct she'd cultivated in medical school and during her internship at Shands whispered that he was sinking.

Activity around the table intensified as the line wavered and flattened. "Quick . . . he's fading!" she read on Josh Reidy's lips.

The injection of an intravenous stimulant had no effect. The heart was Aaron's province. Desperate, he tried electrical stimulus. It was still no go. An incision had already been made in Lin's chest to drain internal bleeding and Aaron followed quickly with open heart massage. The seconds spun out like hours, each minute an eternity. Enormous beads of sweat broke out on Aaron's forehead.

At last the flat line on the monitor screen lifted in one hesitant bleep, and then another. A pause followed in which it flattened again and Lin's hold on life seemed to grow even more tenuous. Kendra could feel the crushing weight of Aaron's tension as if it were her own.

Live, damn it! Live! she imagined him telling Lin inside his head as his strong, beautifully shaped hands stubbornly squeezed and released the boy's flaccid heart muscle. There was another bleep. Pause. Another. Aaron's pumping motion continued unabated.

Suddenly the boy's heart caught hold of the rhythm, as if relearning a language forgotten during a long sleep. Unsteadily at first but with surprising vigor, it signaled the peaks and valleys characteristic of a living person to the monitoring equipment.

A wave of jubilation, fiercely contained, swept the operating room as tears streamed down Kendra's cheeks. Glancing at her watch, she saw only four minutes had elapsed. It wasn't likely Lin had suffered any additional brain damage from oxygen deprivation.

Aaron's relief was visible in every line of his body. For a split second he shut his eyes as if he were uttering a silent prayer of thanksgiving. Lin wasn't out of the woods yet. But he had a fighting chance.

The surgery to repair Lin's brain and neurological injuries, not to mention the numerous fractures he'd incurred, would consume many hours yet. As Josh Reidy took charge once more, one of the nurses reached over to wipe Aaron's forehead. Kendra turned to Bert Ames.

"What about the other children who came in?" she asked, able to breathe normally again. "Do you have any idea how they're doing?"

The resident director shook his head at the gravity of the situation. "There were some minor injuries, of course. Contusions and broken bones, that sort of thing. Unfortunately, to my knowledge, at least two youngsters were dead on arrival. Another expired on the table a half hour ago. Paul Barnard and Hank Greenfeld are still working on a little girl with a severe head injury in suite A next door."

Kendra remembered the child of whom he spoke. Slender, fine boned, with hair like silk, she'd looked like an effigy princess. Her repressed maternal instincts churning just below the surface, Kendra had felt a wild, irrational impulse to kiss her ashen cheek and heal the hurt. I wish modern medicine was as advanced, as powerful as love, she thought. We wouldn't lose so many precious lives.

"Is there anything I can do to help?" she asked. "I can be scrubbed inside of two minutes...."

Dr. Ames's keen blue eyes took in the strain and exhaustion on her face. "At the moment, there's no need," he said gently. "Every procedure is fully staffed. But your fellow resident on the cardiology team, Jane Heard, is assisting Paul and Hank. If you could hang around for a while, be on call in her place..."

"Of course I will," Kendra responded immediately. "I'll notify the operator."

Shortly afterward a minor emergency erupted on the cardiology floor. The moment she had it under control, Kendra raced back to the teaching gallery. As she expected, the slow, meticulous process of repairing Lin's neurological damage was still under way.

Dr. Ames and the other physicians from the teaching staff who'd watched the boy's life-and-death crisis with her had disappeared. Rustling up a cup of black coffee from the surgeons' lounge, she dragged a straight-backed chair into the gallery and pulled it as close as possible to the window. It was going to be a long vigil.

Three grueling hours later, the last bones were set, the final sutures in place. It was almost 10:00 p.m. As if he were reluctant to let go of the boy for even a minute, Aaron watched as an orderly wheeled him to the recovery room. Pete gave his friend's shoulders a brief squeeze as they headed for the sinks.

Kendra guessed what Aaron was thinking. They'd done everything they could. But it might not be enough. The next eight hours or so would decide. With a sigh, she picked up her empty cup.

As she stepped out into the hall, she heard the sound of weeping coming from the family waiting room. Glancing inside, she saw Hank Greenfeld and Jane Heard trying to comfort a sobbing Vietnamese couple. The little girl's parents, she thought, her heart catching in her throat. Looks like she didn't make it.

Hugging herself in an attempt to ease the cold, sick feeling that assailed her, she leaned against the hall's green-tiled apron. It wasn't even her case. Yet despite her training, she'd never gotten over the fact that life was so fragile. One minute a patient was still alive; the next, he or she wasn't.

With children it was especially difficult. The little Vietnamese girl's death had hit her in the place where her inability to have a child was an ever-present regret.

"Redhead?" Aaron asked, tilting her chin upward so that she met his eyes. "Are you okay?"

She'd never seen him look so worn, so weary. The stubbly beginnings of a beard only emphasized the emotional and physical exhaustion he surely felt. How I love him! she thought. More every minute. He's the most special man in all the world.

"I'm all right," she said. "What about Lin?"

Visibly his weariness deepened. "We won't know for a while yet. Care to walk down to recovery with me? I want to take another quick look at him before I call the Morngs."

In the recovery room Lin lay motionless as a wax doll. Even though his oxygen-assisted breathing was faint, it was fairly regular. Tubes and wires connected him to a battery of machines. Both his arms were immobilized in casts. His head and chest were swathed in bandages.

"Any paralysis?" Kendra whispered, half afraid to ask.

"It's probably some kind of minor miracle, but Josh doesn't seem to think so. As for motor control, we'll have to wait and see. It might be quite a while before he regains consciousness."

Satisfying himself that Lin's heartbeat was everything he could hope for at the moment, Aaron ushered Kendra out of the room. "I've got to call the Morngs," he repeated. "And check to see if Troon's still awake. Afterward, you can fill me in on what happened to the other children who were on that bus."

As Kendra expected, Troon was already asleep. She told Aaron what she knew of the death toll over more black coffee in the surgeons' lounge after he'd made his call. Except for them, the big, softly lighted room with its cushioned leather chairs and sofas was deserted. At her news he buried his face in his hands.

He's had a lot of practice at grieving the loss of strangers, she thought. "You haven't had anything to eat for hours, Aaron," she reminded, longing to put her arms around him. "If you like, I can run down to the coffee shop and get you something." It didn't occur to her that she hadn't eaten for the same length of time.

"Thanks," he answered, raising his head. "I don't have much appetite."

By then it was going on 11:00 p.m. Slightly more than an hour remained of his birthday. If she counted the time she'd watched him labor in surgery, they'd spent most of it together.

She knew Lin's recovery was the only present he'd ever want. But right now he needed sleep. "Let me drive you home, then," she suggested. "You ought to get some rest."

His look told her that was an impossibility. "I can't bear to leave him," he explained. "I know it's highly irregular and people will talk. But I need you, Redhead. Stay here with me tonight."

Chapter Eight

They hadn't spent the night together since she'd taken shelter in his bed six years before. She'd been the needy one then, the one who was aching. And he'd cared for her—like a counselor and a friend, almost like a lover who'd willingly put aside any thought of lovemaking for her sake. Now, though he'd done everything he could, he was worried Lin wouldn't make it through the night. Left to his own devices, he'd probably pace or stare red eyed into the darkness.

If she stayed, maybe he'd get some rest. "Of course I will, Aaron," she said.

They kicked off their shoes. Kendra was still wearing her clothes from the accident scene beneath a borrowed lab coat. He'd changed into clean scrubs following Lin's operation. Noting that they wouldn't be the first physicians to spend at least part of the night in the lounge when a patient's life hung in the balance, Aaron dug some utilitarian-looking but soft wool lap robes out of a closet.

"I'll just let the operator know we're here," he said, picking up the phone.

With the hospital switchboard duly informed of his whereabouts, they made themselves as comfortable as possible. Kendra pillowed her head on the arm of a masculine-looking brown leather club chair. A sofa made of the same heavy leather squeaked as Aaron stretched out his tall frame. With a yawn that testified eloquently to his weariness, Aaron shut his eyes. Realizing he needed her presence more than he needed to talk, Kendra did the same.

Somehow she must have drifted off to sleep. When she opened her eyes again, her watch showed a quarter to two. Thanks to the air conditioning and a dearth of bodies, the surgeons' lounge was chilly. Though the room was deadened by acoustic tile to everything but the paging system, she imagined she could hear the faint hum emanating from the hospital's huge physical plant.

Aaron was curled up on his side, his long legs awkwardly accordioned into the available space. His lashes lay sooty and almost childlike against his cheeks, suggesting a vulnerability that contrasted sharply with his stubble of beard. It appeared that he was dozing. He's so wiped out, she thought, shaking her head at the grueling hours of surgery he'd put in after a full day's work. Maybe I can sneak out of here without disturbing him and check on Lin.

Though she made barely a sound as she sat up and started to slip on her shoes, his eyes flickered open. He stared at her for a moment as if he found it difficult to get his bearings. "What time is it?" he asked.

She told him.

"Let's go have a look at Lin," he said.

In terms of the coding used on patient charts, Lin's condition remained critical. He was still unconscious, his breathing still shallow, as if he had a tenuous hold on the physical world.

Yet Kendra could sense something, an improvement so slight, so ephemeral that it defied any attempt to pin it down in words. "I think he's a little better," she whispered. "I can't point to any one thing. But that's how it feels."

Aaron gave her a swift, unreadable look. "I know what you mean," he answered. "I hope it isn't just wishful thinking."

When they returned to the surgeons' lounge, the institutional-size coffee urn, which had rested on a side table, had disappeared. No doubt it had been spirited away for cleaning by the skeleton crew that manned the hospital kitchens at night. Ducking back out to raid the pot in Surgical Intensive Care, they returned to the quiet, softly lighted ambience where they'd previously managed to grab a few winks of sleep.

Neither of them seemed to feel like sleep at the moment. Cradling her disposable cup in both hands for the warmth it provided against the cold draft of the air conditioning, Kendra sensed Aaron felt like talking. But she didn't think he'd want to rehash Lin's case unnecessarily. Like any number of physicians she knew, he seemed vaguely superstitious about doing so while the outcome was still in doubt.

"You know," she remarked, snuggling a little deeper beneath her lap robe, "I've been wondering about something."

One of his brows lifted, inviting her to ask.

"Your knowledge of the Khmer language. And your involvement with the Southeast Asian community. It strikes me you might have been involved in the Vietnam War."

Aaron didn't answer right away. For reasons he didn't fully understand, he'd never volunteered the story that had become part of his distant past to anyone in St. Petersburg except for the Morngs and the refugee association. When he'd founded the clinic, he'd been content to let his colleagues at the hospital think he was eccentric, a bit of a bleeding heart, perhaps even speculate that he was making amends for past sins. Offering basic health care to the city's low-income, shy but exceedingly proud Southeast Asian refugees in a setting where they'd feel comfortable to ask questions about their treatment had been all that mattered to him.

But he didn't mind if Kendra knew. In fact, he wanted to tell her. The story would help her understand why he wanted to adopt Lin and Troon.

"When I was nineteen," he said, "I took a semester off from college to travel and I got zapped by the draft. The army trained me as a medic and sent me to Vietnam. It was bearable at first if you can use a term like that to describe what went on over there.

"Anyway, along came the Tet offensive. I was wounded...a sniper got me in the thigh. I found myself barely able to walk, in pain, behind enemy lines. I stood a good chance of being captured and marched off to a prison camp by the Vietcong.

"Some kids found me...a ragtag, undernourished bunch of boys who probably didn't have a living set of parents between them. They were tough little criminals who existed by stealing. They didn't have a permanent place to lay their heads.

"You know what people say about that war...that everyone was the enemy. Supposedly you couldn't trust a soul, no matter how innocent or friendly they might seem. Well, those boys saved me. They hid me from the Cong and fed me with whatever they could scrounge even if that meant they'd go hungry themselves. They even brought me stuff for bandages so I could dress my wound.

"When some guys from my unit returned to the area, they helped me make contact. They never asked for anything and I didn't have a tangible way of thanking them. I vowed that if I ever got the chance I'd find some way to repay the debt."

When she'd asked him about Vietnam, Kendra had half expected him to tell her he'd fathered (and lost track of) a child over there. Emotionally, she'd been prepared for it. And, though it might have caused her to feel even more strongly that his desire for a son or daughter of his own shouldn't be thwarted, it wouldn't have made her love him less.

Now that she knew what had actually happened, she was deeply moved. She wanted to get up from her chair and put her arms around him. The thought that Aaron had been in danger, wounded and unable to get medical help, was almost unbearable to her though it had taken place many years earlier.

"Was that experience part of the reason you became a doctor?" she asked softly.

He nodded. "Fat lot of good it did me today where some of those children at the scene were concerned. But maybe Lin..."

"I have a feeling you saved Lin's life," Kendra said.

He didn't answer and she speculated he was reluctant to jinx the boy's recovery by agreeing with her. "You forgot to tell me where you learned to speak Khmer," she reminded him. "Did you see action in Cambodia, too?"

Aaron rotated his head to relieve some of the stiffness in his neck. "No," he said. "I've never been there. I picked up my knowledge of the language in Thailand. I was assigned to a base hospital there after my leg healed. From one of the Thai orderlies I learned of a nearby camp for Cambodians who'd fled over the border to escape the Khmer Rouge. I used to go there when I was off duty...volunteer my services. That's where I learned to speak Khmer. It's probably where the idea to found a clinic someday got started, too."

They checked on Lin again at about 4:00 a.m. As defined by alertness or the lack thereof, his condition hadn't changed. Yet again Kendra got the feeling that, despite the boy's pallor and motionless state, he was gathering strength to make a comeback.

They were due to start morning rounds at 6:30 a.m. When they stepped out into the hall, Aaron suggested they go to his place, shower and have breakfast. "I think it's safe to leave him for a little while," he said.

Kendra hesitated. They'd probably overstepped the bounds of propriety already by arriving at the accident scene together, then spending the night in the lounge.

"Do you think that's wise?" she asked, hating herself. "We're bound to be criticized if someone sees us coming out of your house together at 6:00 a.m."

She knew it wasn't an auspicious time to lecture him about professional ethics. His gaze narrowed, his patience with the rigid code of conduct that ruled their lives clearly wearing thin. "Let them," he answered shortly. "We aren't going to do anything they couldn't sell tickets to see."

Though she was practically falling asleep on her feet, Kendra didn't back down. "I don't know about you," she said, trying to make a joke of it. "But I don't want an audience when I'm showering."

Aaron's mouth curved despite the weariness and aggravation he felt. Incredibly, she was learning how to deal with his occasional bursts of irascibility. *How about an audience of one?* he wanted to ask. But he didn't dare. It would only escalate his need for intimacy with her.

"You're right," he conceded, paying reluctant tribute to her sense of humor. "It wouldn't do. I'm glad at least one of us still has their head screwed on straight. C'mon, I'll drive you to the clinic so you can pick up your car."

By the time they met again at the hospital, Lin had been moved to SICU. "Don't quote me, but I think he's better," one of the recovery-room nurses said, stopping to speak with them for a moment before she went off duty. "His lashes fluttered a couple of times. I have a feeling he's about ready to wake."

Scrutinizing the boy's delicate, unmoving features, Kendra got the same impression. The Morngs, who'd paid a brief visit to Lin the night before while he was still in the recovery room, had left word they'd be back sometime before noon. That might do the trick. Frequently patients made an effort to regain consciousness if somebody they knew or cared about was standing beside their hospital bed.

But maybe we don't have to wait for the Morngs, she thought suddenly. By now, Troon's probably awake.

"What would you say to bringing Troon down to SICU to visit Lin?" she asked Aaron. "I know it's against regulations. But he's probably worried sick. And it may be just what Lin needs to fight his way back to us."

Aaron agreed. Now ambulatory, Troon was standing in the doorway of his room, anxiously awaiting word of his erstwhile playmate. He greeted Aaron with a flood of Khmer. Kendra caught Lin's name several times.

Though the Cambodian language was totally beyond her ken, she could tell from Aaron's tone that he was reassuring Troon. She guessed he was probably also giving the boy a quick explanation of what it meant to be unconscious so he wouldn't become alarmed if his little friend didn't speak or move.

Troon wasn't up to climbing stairs yet so they took him up via the elevator in a wheelchair. His dark eyes grew wide and frightened as Kendra held open the heavy SICU door and Aaron pushed him inside. It was obvious he'd never been in such a place. He appeared stunned by the hushed intensity of the nurses and the number of critically ill children in their glass cubicles crammed with life-saving equipment.

"He's over there." Though she spoke in English, Kendra turned Troon's head gently with her hand so that he would look where she was pointing.

The wheelchair wouldn't fit beside Lin's bed so Troon got shakily to his feet. They steadied him as he entered his friend's cubicle. It seemed that the greater part of Aaron's counseling would go for naught. "Lin...Lin!" Troon exclaimed in a panic-stricken voice, clutching the sleeve of his hospital gown and adding something in Khmer that Kendra guessed might translate roughly as "Are you all right? *Please!* Wake up and talk to me!"

There was a moment of silence in which Lin lay like a statue, unmoving and apparently unaware of their presence. Then, for the first time since they'd found him on the bus, he stirred of his own volition. His lashes fluttering as the recovery-room nurse had described, his eyes opened. Before he shut them again, there was a look of recognition in them. Almost a smile.

* * *

For at least twenty-four hours afterward, they were walking on air. Lin seemed to improve by the minute; each time Kendra stopped in to see him, he was a little brighter, a little stronger. Josh Reidy, the neurologist, was even making cautious predictions that his speech and motor ability wouldn't be permanently affected.

A local television station chose to follow its reporting on the accident with the story of his recovery. Alone in her apartment in front of the TV the evening after their all-night vigil, Kendra took a great deal of pleasure in the upbeat account of Lin's progress. Insofar as she could tell, the fresh-faced woman reporter didn't get a detail wrong. She ended by tugging at a few heartstrings with her account of Lin's refugee status and orphaned state.

Two days later Kendra was surprised to see someone other than the Morngs visiting the boy. She guessed the portly, fiftyish man in horn-rimmed glasses and a polyester suit was from the refugee association. But who were the man and woman in their thirties who'd accompanied him? Apparently they were Cambodian; she overheard an exchange in Khmer as she edged closer while checking on another patient. Yet to her knowledge Lin didn't have any living relations.

Aaron caught up with her in the transcription room. "What's the matter?" she asked at once, alarmed by the fierce look of anguish and helplessness on his face.

"Somebody's applied to adopt Lin."

For a moment her reasoning abilities wouldn't function. That's good, she thought. Isn't it? Seconds later the ramifications of what probably *was* a lucky break for the injured boy hit home. Aaron wants him, she realized. And not just him. He wants *the two of them.* Both he and Troon are going to be heartbroken over this.

"Is their...application being considered seriously?" she asked.

He nodded. "I saw some people in with him this morning and I called the refugee association. The couple in question heard about him on television. They live across the bay, in Sarasota, and they're Cambodian. They have all the right qualifications."

The two of them stared at each other for a moment.

"The hell of it is," he added, clearly unhappy with himself for minding so much, "they'll probably make good parents. Maybe even excellent ones. I have no right to begrudge them the opportunity."

She hesitated. "Is there any chance they might take Troon, as well?"

"No. But, to give them credit, the association directors asked."

Except for Lin's good fortune, she couldn't think of a bright spot in the entire situation. "After everything he's been through, including all the worrying he did over Lin's accident, this is going to be terribly hard on Troon," she sympathized.

"You're damn right it is." Aaron looked as if he'd like to smash his fist through the transcription-room window. "Separating him from Lin will be like driving a stake through his heart. Yet they still won't give me the chance to make a home for him."

Somehow they'd have to break the news. Aaron decided they should wait until after they'd attended a group funeral for the children who'd died in the accident. It would be held that afternoon.

Though he seldom put in a personal appearance at patient wakes, preferring to grieve his losses in private, he'd agreed to be present for this one and asked Kendra to accompany him. There wasn't any way Dr. Ames or any of their colleagues could object. Morng Ny had relayed a message from the bereaved parents of the three Cambodian youngsters who had died, thanking them for what they'd tried to do at the accident scene and inviting them to participate.

They'd arranged to leave early, relegating their responsibilities to two of the other cardiology residents. Tense over how she might react, Kendra did her best to dress inconspicuously. Choosing a plain navy outfit, she fastened her unruly hair in a heavy knot at her nape.

Aaron was handsome and sober looking in a tailored charcoal suit when he picked her up at her apartment. She could tell that, like her, he was dreading the service. "At least this is one occasion when they can't accuse us of fraternizing just because we're together," he remarked bitterly as he settled her in his car.

In their own country, Kendra had learned, most Cambodians were Buddhists. However, on coming to the United States, many of them had converted to Christianity. The parents who had lost their children in the school bus accident were typical. They had decided to hold the funeral at a storefront mission church that served as a social and religious center for the city's Cambodian community.

As they walked in, Kendra's heart contracted at the sight of the row of three small gray coffins banked with flowers. Though the service was a traditional, Westernized ritual with Christian hymns and prayers, old cultural customs apparently ran deep. The grieving parents had arranged for Buddhist cremation rites. They'd also set out dishes of fruit and sweets.

"What are those for?" Kendra whispered.

"They're supposed to ease any lingering unhappiness or regret that could keep these little ones tied to the physical world," Aaron explained, the anger and hurt he felt over the children's deaths all too evident. "The idea is to help their spirits soar."

Closing the caskets was a tearful affair. To Kendra it seemed wrong, contrary to the flow of life somehow, to shut the lids on youngsters who hadn't really lived at all. Knowing it would only make Aaron feel worse if she lost it, she managed to confine herself to a few tears.

Following the service, everyone was invited to the Mango Tearoom, which for once had a Closed sign in its window. Wearing a printed sarong with a loose overblouse that failed to hide her advancing pregnancy, Ny served tea. For the most part, Khmer was spoken. Kendra sat on the fringe of the conversation, unable to vent her feelings in words.

At last it was time to go. They weren't scheduled back at the hospital until the following morning. Meanwhile, the evening stretched in front of them, empty yet filled with regret—an evening in which she needed to be with Aaron if only in a quiet way. With the accident victims and Lin's pending adoption on his mind, he probably needed her company, too. Unfortunately, the strictures imposed by her residency were still firmly in place.

Would they be justified in circumventing them, just this once? The successful completion of her residency was a high priority in her life. But Aaron's welfare came first, despite her belief that they could never share anything permanent.

"I make a pretty mean Cincinnati chili," she noted as they turned onto her street. "If you'd care to come up for a little while, I happen to have some in the freezer. It wouldn't take very long to heat."

Though he threw her a surprised look, he didn't point out the inconsistency between her invitation and her refusal to clean up at his house the morning after the accident. Instead he simply helped her out of the car and followed her up the rickety exterior staircase that led to her door.

Tofu rubbed against her ankles as they went inside. She stopped to pet him and open a can of cat food. "The kitchen area's too small for you to help," she told Aaron, grabbing up a barbecue-style apron and fastening it around her waist. "Feel free to get comfortable on the couch."

Glancing around with a kind of blunt curiosity to see how she lived, he flopped down in front of the television set. He appeared to give the public television news report he'd selected scant attention. He's brooding over Lin's pending adoption and trying to think of a way to ease the misery Troon will feel over their separation, she realized, melting the frozen block of chili in a battered pan on her tiny, old-fashioned stove. The pain of it is killing him. I wish there was something I could do to help.

Chapter Nine

Though the chili was a gastronomic success, neither of them was very hungry. Just a short time earlier Aaron would have given anything for the chance to enjoy the simplest of pleasures with Kendra—sharing a meal at her place or his, or walking along Coffee Pot Bayou at sunset. Now he couldn't think of anything but Lin's upcoming adoption and the way Troon was going to react.

What will become of him? he wondered, nudging his half-eaten portion aside. He's going to feel like a leftover, a piece of unwanted baggage returning to a home where Lin doesn't live anymore and he's the only "temporary" orphan on the premises. The Morngs are good to him—there's no denying it. But in a few months all eyes will be focused on their new baby.

When he recovered from his injuries, Lin would reside a forty-five minute drive from St. Petersburg. For all practical purposes, he might as well have been moving to the moon. He and the boy who loved him like a brother wouldn't get to see each other.

One thing's certain, Aaron thought. KCCRA isn't going to change its policy and let me adopt Troon. And it doesn't seem likely he'll be the focus of a television piece subtly designed to flush out a set of adoptive parents.

Troon was just a kid who'd been through the hell of refugee camps in Thailand and the loss of his parents. A kid from another culture with greater-than-average medical needs, growing into an awkward, preteen age. None of the above made him particularly adoptable in the popular sense of the word.

Maybe if Aaron could get the Morngs to accept for Troon the financial support he'd tried unsuccessfully to give them for both boys, they'd qualify to adopt him instead. But it wasn't likely they'd change their minds about taking the money. Low-key though it might appear to the casual observer, their pride was formidable. Besides, what Troon needed wasn't charity, however well intentioned. He needed someone who fiercely wanted and needed him....

"Care for anything else?" Kendra asked. "I can make some coffee. And there's some ice cream in the freezer."

"No, thanks." Shaking off his mordant reverie, Aaron pushed back his chair. "I'd better be going," he said, his voice husky and full of regret. "The chili was great. I didn't do it justice. Or you. I just want you to know how much I..."

There was a pause as they both got to their feet. Impulsively he placed a light kiss on Kendra's forehead. "I was going to say I appreciate everything you've done this week," he added. "But *appreciate* doesn't convey the full extent of what's in my heart."

When Kendra arrived at the hospital the following morning, she realized Aaron had come in early. His briefcase was standing open on his desk. But he wasn't anywhere about. Suddenly she guessed where he'd gone. He was telling Troon about Lin's adoption, taking the full brunt of it on his own shoulders.

Racing down the hall, she hesitated in the doorway of Troon's room. His strong, capable fingers fastened on Troon's bony shoulders, Aaron was addressing him in Khmer. As she watched, the boy's dark eyes widened, uncomprehending. He started to protest. Doggedly Aaron went on speaking, his every word filled with sorrow and affection.

Something crumpled in Troon's face. He'd understood. To Kendra's astonishment he didn't cry out or even whimper. He simply turned away, evading Aaron's firm but gentle grasp, and buried his face against the pillows.

Again Aaron spoke. There wasn't any answer. His thin shoulders hunched together as if for protection against the blind and senseless cruelty of the world, Troon refused to listen—even to the tall American doctor he admired so much.

Glancing up, Aaron saw Kendra standing there. "Do me a favor, will you?" he asked in a lacerated tone. "Go out to the nursing station and call Morng Ny. She's the closest thing he has to a mother. Maybe she can find some way to comfort him."

Kendra winced at the pain in his eyes. "Okay."

"Ask her to come straight to the hospital. Tell her I'll pay for a cab."

Despite Aaron's hopes, Morng Ny didn't fare any better. Nothing she said appeared to break through Troon's wall of seeming indifference and isolation. Usually so polite, he turned his back on her and stared fixedly out the window.

"I don't know how to reach him," Aaron admitted to Kendra in frustration as they watched from the open doorway. "I can implant pacemakers and repair valves until the cows come home. But even the most sophisticated surgical technique won't mend a broken heart."

Things didn't get any better as the day progressed. When Aaron offered to take him to see Lin that afternoon, Troon only shook his head. The nurses on his floor reported worriedly that he was leaving his meals untouched.

To Aaron's chagrin, several months earlier he'd agreed to travel to his alma mater, Johns Hopkins Medical School, for a forum on new surgical techniques. He was scheduled to fly to Maryland at the end of the week. To make matters worse, one of his sisters lived in the Baltimore area. They rarely saw each other and he'd promised to spend a few days with her.

"Take care of Troon, will you, Kendra?" he said the morning of his departure. "I know he's not one of your patients, but..."

She longed to put her arms around him, if only for a moment. "That goes without saying, Aaron," she answered gently. "There wasn't any need to ask."

The day after he left, Ny suffered some breakthrough bleeding. Seeing her in Aaron's stead, Lucy warned her to take it easy, and stressed that she shouldn't try to visit Troon for a few days. Though Kendra didn't know him well and couldn't even speak his language, she became Troon's sole bulwark against a rapidly worsening bout of depression.

I've got to do something, she thought on Wednesday, at her wit's end. No matter how drastic or offbeat it is. Abruptly an idea popped into her head. Though she doubted Aaron would approve, she decided to give it a try. It was her half day off and Lucy didn't expect her at the clinic until late. The man she loved wasn't due back to work until Thursday morning, so she'd have a clear field.

Ny seemed quite surprised to see her when she knocked on the door of the Morngs' apartment above the restaurant. But it didn't take her and the Cambodian woman long to reach an understanding, thanks to Houm's services as translator.

"Ny say your idea good...maybe work," he told Kendra with a smile.

Returning home to her apartment, she gave Tofu a special treat and brushed his snow-white fur until it glistened. Satisfied that he looked his best, she placed him inside a wicker picnic hamper that she'd lined with a towel. A litany of outraged meows accompanied her journey back to the hospital.

Luckily for her, the disgruntled kitten had vented most of his ire by the time they made their way in through a side door and up to the cardiology floor via the back stairs.

"What have you got there—a picnic lunch?" Aaron's rough velvet voice inquired at her elbow just as she was about to start for Troon's door.

She practically jumped a foot. "What are *you* doing here?" she croaked.

He was wearing shorts and a polo shirt and he looked absolutely wonderful. "I grabbed an early flight and decided to check on my favorite patient," he said. "Aren't you going to answer my question?"

Before she could come up with an explanation that might throw him off the track, Tofu let loose with an exasperated yowl.

Aaron's mouth dropped open. "Your *kitten's* in there!" he exclaimed, lifting the hamper lid. "Damn it, Kendra.... Do you really think a visit from Tofu is going to make Troon feel any better about things?"

Annoyed at being caught in the act, she all but snapped at him. "Of course I don't! I'm not taking Tofu to visit Troon. I'm *giving* the kitten to him. I spoke with Ny and Houm and they agreed—Troon can keep him at their place."

Flabbergasted at her generosity, Aaron longed to sweep her off her feet. But even if he'd dared, he wouldn't have been quick enough. Understandably reluctant to part with her pet and determined to get it over with as quickly as possible, Kendra had pushed past him to Troon's bedside. A moment later she was removing the disoriented kitten from the hamper and thrusting him into Troon's arms.

For the first time since he'd learned of Lin's pending adoption, the shutters of abandonment and heartache lifted in the boy's eyes. But he obviously didn't understand the significance of Kendra's gesture.

Aaron had followed her into the room. "Tell him Tofu is an orphan like him, that he needs a friend," she demanded, turning to him. "Ask Troon if he'll please adopt him."

Full comprehension of what she was trying to do dawned on Aaron's face. "I get it," he said. "If we can't comfort Troon, we give *him* a chance to be the comforter."

"Ask him," Kendra repeated.

She held her breath as he translated. His eyes suspiciously bright, Troon nodded in the affirmative. Purring like the finely tuned engine of a miniature BMW, Tofu nestled against his chest. He seemed to recognize a new owner's touch.

Though the presence of pets was forbidden by hospital policy and Aaron was known for his strict interpretation of the rules where patient welfare was concerned, for once he made an exception. Shaking his head at Kendra's ingenuity, he phoned the clinic. When Lucy told him no one had come in yet requiring their level of expertise, they tarried nearly half an hour in the boy's room.

Inevitably Tofu's curiosity got the better of him and he wriggled free, determined to explore. They exchanged warm glances as the kitten's rambunctious behavior elicited several tentative smiles from his new owner. At last, explaining to Troon that Ny would feed and care for his pet until he was released from the hospital, they put Tofu back in the hamper and said goodbye.

A few minutes later they were dropping Kendra's former pet off at the Morngs' restaurant along with a month's supply of cat food. There was a brief exchange of Khmer between Ny and Aaron. Holding Tofu in her arms, Ny waved goodbye as they drove away.

"What did she say?" Kendra asked, observing that Aaron's heart seemed light for the first time since the Sarasota couple had announced their intention of adopting Lin.

He threw her a look. "She said you're a good woman, that I should hang on to you."

A little stab of pleasure knifed through her, though she believed what Ny apparently envisioned for them was an impossibility. "Really?" she asked, striving for a casual air. "What did you answer?"

The tense lines that had bracketed Aaron's mouth so frequently of late relaxed into a teasing smile. "I told her there wasn't anything I could do about it until next summer," he admitted. "And that, in any event, you'd probably be as difficult to catch as a pig on ice. But the truth is, I'm hoping to manage it someday."

Kendra didn't trust herself to speak. They were in the convertible and, her heart spilling over with might-have-beens, she let her windblown hair hide the sudden tears that welled up in her eyes. To every indication, Aaron was learning to care for her, just as she cared for him. With each day that passed their relationship grew more necessary, more profound. Bit by bit, despite the barrier of professional ethics, they were weaving a bond that went far deeper than mere sexual attraction, though an overwhelming desire for each other was its brightest thread.

I love him so much, she thought. And I want him, more than I ever knew it was possible to want anyone. But it can never be. Allowing Aaron to court me wouldn't be fair to him. Lost in her thoughts, she didn't hear what he was saying as they pulled in to the hospital parking lot, and he had to repeat himself.

"Listen up," he prodded. "Lucy claims there isn't much doing at the clinic. Whatever turns up, I'm sure we can handle it. I want you to take the rest of the afternoon off...do something for yourself. You've been running yourself ragged and you deserve a break."

Despite her protests, she could say nothing to change Aaron's mind. Watching him drive off in the Mustang, Kendra didn't notice the muscular male nurse with a military tattoo on his forearm who was arriving in time for the three-to-midnight shift. But he noticed her.

"Mrs. Jenkins!" he said, detouring to speak to her. "So it really *is* you."

Turning distractedly, she had to admit she didn't recognize him.

"Steve Vondracek," he supplied. "I used to work for your husband at Macdill before...well, before his accident. I'm real sorry about that, ma'am. We all were."

Kendra blinked. Caught up in her worries about Troon and her feelings for Aaron, she hadn't thought about Glenn in ages. "Thanks," she said. "I'm pretty much over it now. How've you been?"

The former master sergeant grinned. "Fine. I retired from the service a couple of months ago and I'm working at Bayport now. You?"

"After Glenn's death I went to medical school. I'm a resident next door."

Her late husband's former co-worker beamed in admiration. "Hey, that's great! I've got to hand it to you. Well, guess I'd better run or I'm gonna be late. See you around."

He was halfway to the Bayport entrance when Kendra turned and ran after him. "Listen," she said, "I wonder if you could help me. After Glenn died I tried to locate the woman he was seeing. I wanted to offer her some help if she needed it... you know, for the baby. But I couldn't locate her. Since you used to work with her, I thought you might know something."

Obviously embarrassed by her straightforward reference to what had once been an awkward, hushed-up situation, Steve Vondracek tried to think. "I might have some idea," he said finally. "Last I heard, she lived in the Hibiscus Apartments near the base. But she didn't have a phone. If you want to reach her this afternoon, you might try the Star of Siam grocery on South Dale Mabry. It's a mile or so north of the main gate."

Arn Song, Kendra thought as Steve Vondracek disappeared into the Bayport building. Maybe I'll be able to find her at last. For some reason, the lilting, foreign-sounding name of her late husband's former mistress didn't evoke the sharp pain of betrayal and jealousy it once had.

She had the rest of the afternoon off and Aaron had told her to do something for herself. Yet, out of the blue, finding Song and offering to assist the child Glenn had left behind had become invested with sudden urgency. Not quite understanding her own precipitousness, Kendra got into her car and headed for Gandy Bridge.

She didn't have much difficulty locating the small Thai grocery Steve Vondracek had mentioned. As she parked in its sandbur-choked lot, something in her longed to turn tail and run. But she couldn't. Though fate had given Song the opportunity to bear a child it had denied to her, the question of that child's welfare had always haunted her.

She got out of the car and went inside. "I'm looking for someone named Arn Song," she told the woman behind the counter.

"I Song," the woman said.

Kendra stared. She knew Glenn's former mistress was about her own age. Yet the scrawny clerk in her dark cotton jacket and faded sarong appeared to be at least ten years older. Could the sad-looking, careworn human being who faced her from behind the cash register with a polite inquiry on her face really be the woman whose presence in Glenn's life had caused Kendra so much pain?

She swallowed. "I'm Glenn Jenkins's wife... or rather his widow," she said at last. "I've come to talk to you about your baby."

Astonishment and confusion warred with shame on the Cambodian woman's face. "Mrs. Jenkins," she stammered. "I so very sorry about what happen. I not know until after Glenn die that he have a wife."

Kendra was astonished, too. She didn't answer.

"When I find out," Song went on earnestly, "I feel bad. But it already too late. Baby coming..."

Kendra nodded, still not knowing what to say. "Your child must be..." she whispered.

"Five year old."

Despite her deep embarrassment, a note of pride crept into Song's surprisingly girlish voice. She's a good mother, a loving mother, Kendra guessed. And she's fortunate to have had that opportunity, even with the hardships she must face.

"How do you live?" she asked without thinking how inquisitive the question must sound. "This job must not pay you very much."

It was a direct request for sensitive personal information on the part of a stranger and something closed in Song's face. Then, "Not easy," she admitted. "But better than in my country under Khmer Rouge."

Song's translation to a flesh-and-blood human being who hadn't meant her any harm wasn't to be Kendra's only watershed experience that afternoon. She caught her breath as the rickety screen door of the grocery creaked open and a small boy came in. Golden skinned like Troon and Lin, with dark, almond-shaped eyes and streaks of blond in his silky, straight brown hair, he'd obviously been playing in the dirt. His hands, so dusty, small boned and perfect, reminded her of butterfly wings.

Kendra guessed immediately that he was Glenn and Song's son. Darting a quick look at her, he ran shyly to his mother's side.

"This is Pran," Song said diffidently but with obvious pride. "He good boy. Worth shame I feel when I find out truth about his father."

Driving back across the bay, Kendra felt as if a weight had been lifted from her shoulders. She no longer blamed Song for what had happened. In fact, she felt sorry for her. As she headed toward the somber, slate blue clouds of a gathering thunderstorm, she decided that the proceeds from at least one of Glenn's insurance policies, currently gathering interest in a certificate of deposit, would be converted to a trust with his son as beneficiary.

She'd set it up so Song received monthly interest payments for the boy's support. Pran would be given the principal to use for college or whatever he wanted on his eighteenth birthday.

Lightning flashed over the St. Petersburg shoreline, splitting the sky horizontally and briefly illuminating the television towers near the dog track. At that moment she realized her envy of Song's ability to have a child hadn't completely disappeared. If I had that ability, she thought, I'd be looking forward to the time when Aaron and I could be together instead of planning to move away when my residency is completed. We could marry and adopt Troon together.

But maybe they could still be man and wife, at least long enough to accomplish that.

It had been her afternoon for coming to the aid of children though she could never have any of her own. And it occurred to her that, if she were willing to forget the emotional cost and live with love just out of reach for a little while, maybe Aaron could have his wish.

She didn't harbor any illusions that giving her kitten to Troon had permanently solved the boy's problems. It had pulled him out of his downward spiral, at least for the time being. But his depression was all too likely to return when Lin's adoption became a fact and the Morngs concentrated their attention on the new baby.

I wish Troon could be my son, too, she thought. I've grown fond of him, particularly during the past several weeks. I really think I could be a good mother to him. Although she could never allow herself to seize that opportunity on a permanent basis, perhaps she *could* give him and Aaron the gift of a lifelong father-son relationship.

If her plan worked, they'd be deceiving the refugee committee. But they'd be doing so in a good cause. The more she thought about it, the more she felt unconventional, even drastic means were justified. As Aaron had once put it, Troon's childhood was going by in the blink of an eyelash.

It was raining buckets by the time she pulled in to the clinic parking lot. Aaron and Lucy were just locking up.

"What're you doing here?" he asked, bolting through the downpour and getting into her car on the passenger side. "I thought I told you to get some rest."

His hair was wet, the polo shirt he wore literally plastered to his skin. To her, drenched, dripping and a little put out with her, he was still the most beautiful man on earth. Gazing into his amber eyes at such close range was enough to make her have second thoughts. The plan she was about to suggest would be doubly difficult to carry out because of the way she loved him.

Love is what inspired the idea. And love would help her see it through. "I have a proposal for you," she said at last. "I think we should get married...now...if we can obtain Dr. Ames's and the board's blessing. Surely some way can be found to deal with the nepotism problem fairly and equitably. Once the deed is done, the refugee association won't have any further reason to turn down your application."

Aaron stared at her in astonishment. He was certain he'd misunderstood. "You're...actually serious about this?" he said after a moment.

She nodded. "Troon needs you."

He reached for her then. "Ah, Redhead," he growled, his face against her hair. "Troon needs us both. We need *each other.* Don't you know it's what I've wanted since you first came back to St. Petersburg?"

It was such a luxury just to let him hold her. Heaven to think he wanted her the way she wanted him. The fact that you can't have a child need not matter, she tried to convince herself. Maybe it isn't the most important thing in the world.

As clearly as if he'd repeated them while he held her in his arms, she remembered his words the evening she'd brought him home from the airport. *Like most men,* he'd said with every appearance of sincerity, *I'd like to marry and father a child someday.* It was a highly understandable wish.

If she told him the truth, he'd pretend it didn't matter. That's how he was. Better a brief, sharp wound than a lifetime of regret.

"Please, Aaron," she protested, pulling back from him a little. "You don't understand."

He frowned as if an inkling of what she was contemplating had somehow crossed his mind. "You asked me to marry you," he replied. "And I accept... provided your residency isn't adversely affected. What's so complicated about that?"

If they were to save Troon, if Aaron was to have his wish, she couldn't falter. "I'm not suggesting we live together as man and wife," she whispered, knowing how much it would hurt him. "Just that we marry temporarily until Troon's position is secure."

Chapter Ten

Predictably, he was angry. And just as predictably, hurt. "Are you trying to tell me you don't love me?" he demanded with all the ferocity of a thunderclap, as rain streamed down the windshield. "That you'd be doing this just for him?"

If she lived to be a hundred, she could never tell him that. "I'm offering to do it for both of you," she said. "I...*care* for you both, very much."

"Then what's this nonsense all about?" Urgent and powerful, his hands gripped her shoulders. "If Bert Ames and the board approve, why can't we have a real marriage? What could possibly stop us from making love to each other?"

It was the one question she couldn't answer, the crux of their whole miserable situation. "I have my reasons," she responded helplessly. "I can't explain."

He swore at that, stringing expletives together so furiously she wanted to cringe from the onslaught. "Know what I think?" he added, getting out of the car without making any effort to protect himself from the cloudburst. "You're crazy. I wouldn't marry you under those terms if you were the last woman on earth."

That night, tossing in his double bed, Aaron went over their painful confrontation. Kendra had hit him where he lived, raising the cup of fulfillment to his lips and then dashing it aside. He wanted to throttle her. Yet by now he'd realized she was hurting, too. He just couldn't fathom why she felt the way she did.

I thought we had an understanding, that we were building something rare and wonderful together despite the impossible situation we have to contend with until next summer, he tormented himself. I never dreamed she was still holding on to the reservations she expressed that night on the Bradleys' boat.

Yet rack his brain though he might, he couldn't guess what those reservations were. Just once he'd accused her of not wanting to get stuck with Lin and Troon and he'd been forced to admit how wrong that notion was. Children were her profession, her life, and she clearly loved them. It was obvious she cared deeply about Troon's future. And she'd worried over Lin when his life hung in the balance as if he were her own child.

So, he thought. If it isn't anything to do with having kids underfoot, what can it be? She's healthy; I saw her physical report myself. And there doesn't seem to be a hint of any prior commitment.

No matter how forceful the argument, no one could convince him she didn't share his feelings. Each time he'd held her, crushing her sweetness against his body, he'd sensed the bonfire of her need leaping to meet him, as barbaric and all consuming as his.

On that and one other point—the genuineness of her offer—he had little doubt. For Troon's sake *and* ours, I ought to call her bluff, he told himself, restlessly throwing off the light blanket that covered him and pacing the room. See just how long she can hold out against me.

By morning he'd made up his mind. Kendra and the other cardiology residents were in his office at the hospital, drinking coffee and waiting for him to begin the brief staff meeting he'd called for his return from Maryland, when he arrived. One glance at her and he guessed that, like him, she'd spent a sleepless night.

"Before we get started, Dr. Jenkins," he said, casually taking a seat and drawing the surgery schedule out of his briefcase, "I've changed my mind and decided to go along with your suggestion of yesterday afternoon. To that end, I've made an appointment for us to discuss it with Dr. Ames at four o'clock. Please be prompt."

She was waiting for him in the hall outside the resident director's office at the appointed hour, her eyes still wide with the shock and relief he'd surprised in them earlier. Nervously she pushed back an auburn strand that had escaped from her neat chignon.

"What... made you reconsider?" she asked.

He shrugged. "Like you, I don't think Troon can survive much longer without roots. I'm sure I needn't tell you a patient's mental state can affect his recovery. Or point out that I've postponed Troon's valve surgery until his emotions have stabilized."

Nodding, she hugged her slender arms. "Does this mean you accept the conditions I set?"

He wanted to shake her. "Yes," he answered. "I accept... for as long as you care to enforce them. What do you say we go inside?"

Peering at them over his half glasses, Dr. Ames's eyes held a frosty glint. I have a feeling he's been biding his time—waiting to lower the boom on us until Lin's condition improved and Aaron got back from Baltimore, Kendra thought. She could see convincing him he should relax the rules instead of tightening them wasn't going to be easy.

She decided to let Aaron do most of the talking. He was the one with authority and standing at the hospital. However, it quickly appeared neither would be enough.

"The rules are simple—no nepotism. And no personal relationships between professor and residents," Bert Ames replied when Aaron had finished stating their case. "I expect you to abide by them. Marriage between the two of you now is out of the question if Kendra expects to remain a resident here."

Thanks to the unresolved conflict between him and Kendra, Aaron wasn't feeling very diplomatic. "If she's out, then so am I," he shot back. "But it needn't come to that. Once I resign, you'll have no reason to dismiss her from the program."

The threat didn't go down well. "Don't be too sure of that," Dr. Ames replied. "It's obvious to me you've both broken some rules."

A strained silence filled the room. They'd tried—oh, how they'd tried, to keep their relationship on a professional basis. Though for the most part they'd succeeded, they'd fallen short of the ideal and Kendra knew it. She couldn't fault Dr. Ames for taking them to task.

Aaron was probably thinking similar thoughts.

"You're one of our best professors," Dr. Ames reminded him. "I don't want to lose you. Or Kendra. But my principles aren't subject to compromise. A year from now you can do as you please. Can you afford not to wait?"

In Kendra's opinion, *Troon* couldn't afford it.

"There's something I think you should know, Dr. Ames," she said, prodded into telling him the details Aaron had chosen to omit. "We want to adopt Sem Troon. The refugee association won't give him to us unless we're married. With his best friend spoken for by that Sarasota couple and his foster mother about to direct most of her attention to a new baby, his emotional state is precarious. We feel he needs us now. Next year may be too late."

Frustrated as he was with her, Aaron wanted to take her in his arms. This is going to work out despite her reservations, he told himself. I know it is. She, I and Troon belong together.

She could sense the shift in Aaron's mind-set as Dr. Ames took off his glasses, polished them and walked over to the window. We're in this together, she realized, her feeling of partnership with him a heady one. For perhaps the thousandth time, she tried not to pretend things would always be that way.

With a sigh that bordered on capitulation, Dr. Ames turned to them. "I don't know," he hedged. "I have to admire what you're trying to do. I may even agree with it. But what you're suggesting is highly irregular. Even if I could get the board to agree, I can't honestly see how you'd work out the details."

Tempted to push for a victory, Aaron held himself in check. Despite their best efforts to follow the rules, they'd challenged Dr. Ames's pride and authority. Much could be gained by hearing him out.

"Kendra's dependent on you for her evaluation," the older man continued after a moment. "In light of what you're proposing, what guarantee do we have it would be impartial?"

He was on the verge of giving them a chance! "I've already thought of that," he said, not mentioning that he'd worked out the finer points of his proposal sometime after 3:00 a.m. "If you and the board concur, I'll continue to act as her professor in every way but one—the evaluation of which you speak. When it comes to that, someone qualified like yourself can sit in judgment."

Dr. Ames's "Hmm" was noncommittal. But he didn't refute the point.

"However, if you trust me, I *can* be impartial," Aaron added with a wry smile. "Naturally, I'd be tougher on her than on anyone else in the program."

"You already are!"

The squawk of protest was Kendra's and it carried the day. "From what I've been able to determine, your standards for her are already a little steep." Dr. Ames chuckled. "Tell you what... Put it in writing and I'll present your request to the board when it meets tomorrow evening. Provided the members are willing to grant a dispensation, I'll act as Kendra's official supervisor. If I left her to your tender mercies, I'm not sure she could take the heat."

Three days later, after the board had granted its reluctant approval, they applied for a license and said their vows at the county building with Kim Johanssen and Pete Bradley acting as witnesses. Kendra wore a robin's-egg-blue dress and jacket, Aaron the gray suit she remembered from the Cambodian children's funeral. At Kim's insistence, she carried a nosegay of gardenias. Aaron had a white carnation in his lapel.

They looked so tense, so serious, Kendra was sure Kim and Pete suspected they were having second thoughts. But in truth there hadn't been much time for them. Things had been hectic at the hospital since their session with Dr. Ames, and after speaking with him their only hurdle had been the board. There wasn't any waiting period in Florida. She was stunned, almost light-headed when the deputy clerk of the circuit court pronounced them man and wife.

"You may kiss the bride," the clerk told Aaron, beaming her approval.

As if in slow motion, his arms came around Kendra. He covered her mouth with his. The wedding ceremony that had seemed so arid, so cut-and-dried, blossomed like a flower in time-lapse photography. Dizzily she drank in the scent of the man she loved. She wanted to swoon like the heroine of a Victorian novel at the bold intrusion of his tongue.

I'm going to make it tough on you, he seemed to be saying as he lifted her slightly off her feet. I'm going to make you crave our lovemaking so much that you literally beg for it.

She didn't doubt for a moment that he could. Each nerve ending in her body responding as if it had a will of its own, Kendra imagined him carrying her over the threshold of the Coffee Pot Bayou bungalow and upstairs to his bed. While the rest of the world went about its business, they'd undress each other with loving eyes and hands, move naked into their nuptial embrace. Though she knew it could never be, goose bumps of anticipation feathered over her skin.

As the seconds ticked away, Aaron's kiss only seemed to deepen.

"Hey," Pete protested kiddingly, his voice tinged with sudden embarrassment, "you guys have all day for that. Some of us have to get back to the hospital."

The atmosphere relaxed a little as the four of them shared champagne, salad and Spanish bean soup at Pepin to celebrate. It unwound even more, at least on the surface, once they were alone. They'd taken the entire day off and, seemingly cooperating in the fiction that nothing extraordinary had happened, they donned T-shirts and shorts to move Kendra's few belongings the short distance to his house.

But there was still tension, smoldering in the air.

"Sure this is what you want?" Aaron asked with narrowed eyes when Kendra insisted on placing her clothing and personal items in the bureau and closet that would have been Lin's if Aaron could have adopted him.

"I'm sure."

Though she was adamant, believing she had to be for his sake, the words reverberated in her ears like a lie. She wondered if he could sense the battle that was raging in her heart.

He was standing between her and the door of the medium-size bedroom she'd occupy, which had been furnished with bunk beds and oak stacking units. "Look," he said, "we're husband and wife now. That means you can tell me anything. Isn't it time you explained?"

Though she ached to tell him, longed from the very depths of her soul to hear him say her inability to give him a child didn't matter, she believed he'd only say it out of compassion. She didn't want to trap him that way.

"I'm sorry, that's not possible," she said in a low voice, starting to brush past him. "If you'll excuse me, I have to get—"

His mouth cutting her off in midsentence, he pulled her into his arms. Fierce and oh, so loving, his tongue entered to duel with hers. The way he grasped her buttocks through the seat of her shorts and hauled her against the rigid outline of his need was a blatant invitation.

She couldn't give in to it. Nothing about their situation had changed despite the signed copy of a marriage license Aaron had put away in a bureau drawer. Wrenching free, she faced him with pupils that had widened to pools of velvet against the stormy green of her irises, a chest whose rapid rise and fall betrayed a passion she couldn't quell.

"I told you, Aaron.... We can't!" she whispered.

He stared, not bothering to hide the all-too-prominent evidence of how much he wanted her. "You really mean that, don't you?" he asked.

"Yes. Yes, I do."

Something closed in his face. "Okay, Redhead. Have it your way. But I think you're making a big mistake."

Just how big a mistake she'd made didn't dawn on her until the following day at the hospital, when she stopped by to see Troon. My God, what can I have been thinking of? she moaned to herself. This boy is on such fragile emotional ground. How's he going to feel when he guesses his new adoptive parents are married in name only? Or worse still, if they split up after the adoption is finalized?

A little voice taunted that maybe her motives had been selfish ones. *No,* she thought. That isn't how it was at all. Yet with a sinking feeling she realized her conscience might have a point. Perhaps without knowing it she'd found a back door into marriage with Aaron, subsconsciously creating a diversionary tactic whereby she could stake permanent claim to him before being forced to confess her inability to have his baby.

Oh, please...I wouldn't play with Troon's life like that, Kendra agonized. I only wanted to help him. And Aaron. But the fact was, she'd boxed them into a corner. Seeing a way to adopt Troon and dispense with the ethical problems that had plagued them, Aaron hadn't taken her proviso seriously. The dilemma they were facing wasn't his fault.

What were they going to do?

We'll have to get a divorce, she thought frantically. Or rather an annulment. There are worse things than being a foster child. We can't hurt Troon this way.

But it was already too late. A shy smile lighting his face, Troon was trying to tell her something in Khmer. He produced a picture he'd drawn with his crayons of a man, a woman and a half-grown boy with straight, dark hair. The man and woman were wearing lab coats.

"I told him this morning that we hoped to adopt him," Aaron explained from the doorway. "He gave us his blessing. I've arranged an appointment for us at the agency Wednesday afternoon."

Besieged with guilt and unable to think clearly about what to do, Kendra let go of solutions and allowed herself to drift with events. She felt a deepening fatalism when, after pointing out it wasn't standard procedure for newlyweds to adopt, the refugee association director agreed to look with favor on their application.

It's meant to be, she thought, focusing her mind on matters she *could* deal with, like shopping for furniture and finding a housekeeper. Aaron and Troon were meant to have each other. I'm just the instrument charged with bringing that about.

Of course, she'd have to tell Aaron the truth eventually. And she wasn't looking forward to it. Once Troon has settled in, I'll do it, she promised herself—urge him to decide what we should do based on his feelings, not mine. Regretful she hadn't spilled the beans when she'd proposed to him in the car, or even on their wedding night, she knew separating from him would break her heart.

The day Aaron and Jane Heard performed Troon's valve surgery, Kendra placed a help-wanted ad. They really didn't need a housekeeper until Troon came home. But she felt the presence of another person might defuse some of the tension between her and the husband who still hadn't shared her bed.

Inevitably that tension had spilled over to their work environment. Though Aaron didn't carp and pick on her the way he once had, the relentlessly formal attitude he'd adopted instead hadn't gone unnoticed. Spurred by surprise at their sudden, unorthodox marriage, tongues had begun to wag afresh over what everyone considered their dogged professionalism.

"If I didn't know better, I'd never guess the two of you were newlyweds," Bess commented with a laugh when she and Kendra met for lunch. "I hope for your sake things are cozier around the house."

With all her heart, Kendra wished she could answer yes. But she couldn't. She blushed at what Bess would say if she knew about their situation.

The Wednesday after their visit to the refugee association offices, Kendra conducted interviews with several of the women who'd responded to her ad. The most promising candidate was African-American, middle-aged and widowed with an eight-year-old son. Though the boy was two years younger than Troon and almost certainly didn't speak Khmer, Kendra thought they might be company for each other.

"Part of the job involves looking after a ten-year-old Cambodian boy who doesn't speak any English," she said, explaining the terms of employment. Afterward, she conducted the woman on a tour of the house and showed her the garage apartment. "As I mentioned before, you'll be required to live on the premises. We'll expect you to cook for us. Maybe even learn to prepare some Cambodian-style dishes. It won't be nine to five. You'll be doing a lot more than the standard housekeeping chores."

"That's all right." Rosa Johnson's warm brown eyes sparkled at the challenge. "I *like* looking after kids," she said. "And I'm a terrific cook. The salary you're offering is more than generous. Maybe I shouldn't say this, but I'd stand on my head to get this job if that's what you required."

Kendra tried to imagine such an offbeat situation. "Why so?" she asked, unable to suppress a laugh.

Rosa shrugged. "We've been living with my aunt. The neighborhood isn't the best. Your garage apartment is a godsend. I want Clive—that's my son—to grow up in a better environment."

Troon's surgery was a success, and each day Lin made new strides toward recovery. As Thanksgiving drew near, there was a lot to be thankful for. Meanwhile, Kendra's killing schedule at the hospital didn't abate. Redoubling her efforts so that none of her fellow residents could cry favoritism, she went back to helping out at the clinic, too. Her every spare moment was consumed by whipping the house into shape.

As a result, she fell into bed exhausted each night. Though her routine took an enormous amount of energy, it couldn't smother the longing she felt. Erotic dreams plagued her the minute she closed her eyes.

Aaron hadn't made another move in her direction. Though they acted determinedly casual and matter-of-factly when they teamed up to arrange newly acquired living-room furniture or refinish a pair of bookcases, the tension between them didn't lessen. She kept wanting to rub her cheek against his jaw, wanting to touch him. A thousand times in her imagination she asked him to take her to bed.

Leaving the hospital early one afternoon, since she'd been on call the night before, Kendra inspected and bought a handsome secondhand dining table and chairs she'd located through the classified. As she wrote out her check and promised to have a local moving company pick them up, the usual afternoon thundershowers were threatening.

She was bone weary; the previous night had been a busy one on the cardiology floor. Instead of running around town on a host of trivial errands the way she'd planned, she decided to go home and get some sleep.

Raindrops splattered the windshield as she turned into the driveway and pulled under Aaron's trellised carport. Before long he'd be home. From her bunk in what was to have been Lin's room she'd hear him rustling around, getting an apple out of the refrigerator. And she'd want him, so much her insides would ache.

The strain of living like this is getting to be too much for me, she thought. Something's got to give. Allowing her mind to go blank, she gave her body permission to relax any way it chose. A moment later she was opening the car door and kicking off her shoes. How good that felt! After a quick glance around to make sure nobody was watching, she peeled down her nylons. Tucking them under the seat, she headed barefoot for the miniature jungle of greenery that dominated the back yard.

Aaron had told her the house's previous owners were avid tropical gardeners. Their handiwork was everywhere, expressed in elephant ears and banana plants, palms and other tropical trees. Beneath Kendra's feet the grass was green and lush. She imagined her toes curling down into it, sinking into the earth like roots.

I love Aaron, she thought. I want him and Troon to be part of my life. Maybe if I could come to terms with my childlessness, Aaron could do the same.

Inevitably the light patter of the rain quickened and she ducked into the small, weathered gazebo they'd been meaning to paint. Bemused, she watched as a silvery curtain descended over the landscape.

Like life with Aaron and Troon, the downpour seemed to beckon. I don't want to stay dry, she thought suddenly. I want to feel the rain on my face. Loosening the neat, heavy coil of her hair, she stepped out into the deluge. Quickly her auburn tresses were plastered to her head like seaweed. Her cotton blouse and skirt were soaked through in seconds.

With an abandon that echoed what Aaron could make her feel, she welcomed the torrent. Through it, she stood looking at the house as if she'd never seen it before. Quaint and unassuming with its 1920s craftsman lines, it was also spacious, warm and welcoming—a home in the making she wanted to share. As the rain continued to fall, it mixed with her tears.

"Kendra...sweetheart...what are you doing out here?" His hair clinging in damp points to his forehead and his shirt transparent from the wet, Aaron had arrived and come looking for her.

She didn't need a mirror to know that the deep feelings she had for him were showing on her face. "Looking at your house," she admitted. "Wishing it was *ours*."

She was handing him the opening he'd almost given up hoping for. "Don't you know it has been, from the moment you came back into my life?" he asked, his hands at her waist.

Too emotional to speak, she shook her head.

"Surely you know how much I love you."

He'd never put it in so many words; she'd never let him. More tears flowed. "I only know how much I love you."

As the rain streamed down, his mouth claimed hers. With a little shudder of ecstasy she welcomed it. It's time, *past* time for us, she thought, her need blurring into his. Whatever happens later, at least we'll know what it is to have each other.

Chapter Eleven

Suddenly the barriers that had kept them apart seemed as frangible as cellophane or smoke. Touching, kissing, they steeped themselves in the unexpected luxury of holding each other. Aaron could hardly believe any of it was happening. He was afraid she'd vanish. Or have a change of heart.

"Will you let me love you?" he asked.

"Oh, *Aaron*. Yes..."

"My lovely redheaded wife..."

We'll take each other the way I once imagined, he thought. Curtained by greenery and the little gazebo, on the sweet-smelling grass. Worshiping the curves and hollows of her figure with reverent hands, he drew her toward the secluded nook he'd pictured. Little more than a gap between overhanging leaves, it was invisible to the outside world. Even the housekeeper's apartment where Rosa and her son would soon reside was on the opposite side of the property.

Pulling her down beside him, he nipped gently at her shadowed peaks through the rain-soaked fabric of her blouse.

"Here?" she whispered.

He raised his head to look at her as his fingers went to her buttons. "It's what I've wanted since that night you brought me home from the airport."

Opening his shirt so that she could feel him, too, Kendra rested her head on a springy pillow of clipped St. Augustine lawn. Her breasts uncovered to Aaron's mouth and her skirt pushed up to her waist, she helped him remove her panties. The way he was caressing her caused her womanhood to open like a well.

Moments later he'd unzipped his trousers. Nudging her, teasing her, he sought her feminine mysteries even as he drove her to the brink of consummation.

Hovering there, she moaned with fierce, almost savage pleasure when he entered her. Their wet, partially clad bodies clinging together, she wrapped her legs around him. He paused only briefly to rein in his need before beginning to move. Abandoning what little control she had left, she lifted her hips and bore down with the small of her back to offer herself completely. It was she who capitulated first.

Exceeding the limit of pleasure she thought she could endure, the first real culmination Kendra had ever experienced carried her away. Her cheeks glowed like embers. Gooseflesh covered her thighs. Seconds later, Aaron followed. United by the force of their passion, they brushed past the gates of paradise.

As the rain slowed to a pattern of drips and plops punctuated by bird calls, Aaron gathered her close. "God, but I love you, Kendra Dash," he whispered.

"I love you, too."

She'd never be able to tell him how much. This man, she thought, with his lean, muscular body, high standards and giving heart, is really here in my arms. We've just made love to each other. He's mine to nurture and explore.

When she confessed her inability to have children, maybe he'd understand. She'd beg him if that's what it took. Meanwhile, they had until Thanksgiving. Troon would be released in time for the holiday and—once he was settled—she'd tell Aaron everything. The deadline she'd set for herself seemed very far away.

Nibbling at her ear, he removed a blade of grass from her hair. "Let's go into the house and shower," he suggested. "I want to make love to you again... between smooth, dry sheets."

Decently covered once more, though they looked like hobos emerging from a wrestling match, they stepped out of their bower with their arms about each other.

Showering with Aaron was a new and erotic discovery. Soap slickened and fully naked with him for the first time, Kendra delighted in the wonders of his body. Water streamed as he discovered hers.

They'd wanted each other too long and too desperately for their respite from lovemaking to last. Inevitably things got out of hand again. Though they were smooth and dry to begin with, his sheets didn't stay that way after they'd tumbled dripping into bed.

This time their need wasn't as poignant, as aching, though already it seemed deeper, more profound. Feasting on her with his eyes, Aaron took the time to assume protection. As he did so, he explained that the small, square packet he'd withdrawn from a drawer in his bedside table had been purchased for their wedding night.

Guilt warred with desire as she watched. We don't need contraceptives, she thought. I ought to tell him so. But she didn't have the nerve.

Moments later her thoughts were empty of everything but him. She gasped with delight as he showed her just how talented his hands and mouth could be. Seizing them almost simultaneously, their second culmination was even deeper than the first.

They hadn't turned on either of the bedroom lamps. As the late-afternoon light faded into dusk, Aaron drew her head against his shoulder. "By the way, I want to apologize for what happened earlier," he said.

Alarm coursed through her. Was he sorry they'd consummated their marriage? If so, he wasn't acting...

Sensing the wrong turn her thoughts had taken, he tightened his embrace. "In case you're wondering if I regret making love to you," he added, "the answer is *no.*"

"What are you talking about, then?"

"The way we did it the first time, without protection. I was so carried away, I completely forgot to take responsibility. You could be pregnant. And I don't want that to happen now. You won't be finished with your residency for another eight months...."

Without realizing it, he was giving her another chance to tell him. Sated and still a neophyte when it came to the pleasures of his bed, she couldn't work up the needed courage.

"I wouldn't worry," she replied, kicking herself for what sounded like sheer idiot complacency.

He placed a light kiss against her hair. "If by that you mean it's the wrong time in your cycle, you're much too intelligent to think that's any guarantee. But if you aren't concerned about the possibility, then I'm not, either. We're going to be parents soon, anyway. And though the timing would be inconvenient, I have to admit I rather like the thought of giving you a baby."

Spoken so lovingly, his words left the shining palace of Kendra's hopes in a million glittering shards. Oh, *no,* she agonized. It really does matter to him! All the guilt she felt over not telling Aaron and what would happen to Troon as a result returned a hundredfold. Now that she and Aaron were lovers, she guessed, the truth would hurt him twice as much.

"What's wrong?" he asked as she turned on her side, facing away from him against the pillows.

For a moment she didn't trust herself to answer. Then, "I guess I'm a little tired," she said in a small voice.

He should have realized. Before leaving the hospital, she'd said something about a nap. Fitting himself around her so that they nestled together like spoons, Aaron lifted a heavy, sweet-smelling strand of her hair and kissed her neck. Though they hadn't had supper yet and he was beginning to feel a little hungry, he wasn't going anywhere.

"Get some sleep, Redhead," he murmured, resting one hand lovingly on her hip. "If we feel like eating or a reprise later, we can have a midnight snack."

She couldn't bear to tell him. Not until she must. Maybe it was selfish of her, but she didn't want to give him up any sooner than necessary. Drowning her guilt and apprehension in work and making repeated, fevered love to her new husband, Kendra managed somehow to get through the days and nights.

Rosa moved in, improving their living conditions a hundredfold. With none of the household details to contend with, they had more free time. Kendra bought an English-as-a-second-language guide and used some of hers to teach Troon a few basic words and phrases. It's the least

I can do for him, she thought. Though I likely won't be around in his life for long, I can be a good mother while I have the chance.

Because of Troon's shyness and obvious desire to please her by avoiding mistakes, she wasn't sure if the lessons were having any effect. Yet according to Aaron, who managed to elicit more commentary from Troon than she did, he was making definite progress.

"I'm beginning to think he's learned more English than he's letting on," he commented on one occasion. "Sometimes if he doesn't know the Khmer word for a new concept, he uses the English one."

Inexorably Thanksgiving approached. In one way, Kendra was as eager as Aaron for Troon to come home to them; she'd begun to love him as if he were their own child. Yet in another, she dreaded facing the deadline she'd set for herself. Troon would be irreparably damaged if she and Aaron parted over her duplicity. And now that they were lovers, Aaron would be even more deeply hurt. The longer she kept her secret, it seemed, the more of a problem it became.

To compensate, she planned a huge Thanksgiving feast that would also serve as a welcome party for Troon. Hoping to make the boy feel more at home, she invited Houm and Ny as well as Bess Martin and the Johanssens. She also asked Rosa and Clive to eat with them.

Though he was doing marvelously well, Lin wouldn't be released from the hospital in time for the holiday. Maybe next year he and his adoptive parents will be able to join us, she thought as she used her credit card to buy a complete set of china in Royal Doulton's Kingswood pattern for the occasion. A moment later she remembered that next year was a giant question mark.

* * *

Kendra was worn out from thinking about all the possibilities inherent in their situation by the time Thanksgiving morning arrived. "Umnf..." she murmured, burying her face in the pillows when their alarm buzzer sounded.

A morning person, Aaron was fully awake in an instant. Punching the Off button, he turned to look at his wife. She was still three-quarters asleep, her rump nestled in telltale intimacy against his thigh and her tousled, coppery curls partially obscured by the bedcovers.

How he loved her now. And how he needed her. If anything happened to separate us, he thought, it would be like losing a piece of myself.

Today was the big day. Troon would be coming home and they'd be a family. He was grateful Kendra had learned to love the boy as much as he did. So why did the nagging, formless worry at the back of his mind persist?

The answer was a simple one. Something was bothering her, though she tried to pretend otherwise. Maybe she has qualms over raising a ten-year-old without prior experience as a parent, he thought. If so, it's understandable. But he didn't really believe that was a problem. She was good with children. And she knew it, too.

To all appearances, her reasons for not wanting him to court her once her residency was over and for refusing to sleep with him when they were first married had gone by the board. But had they really? She'd never discussed them with him.

He wondered suddenly if she was pregnant. Since their rash encounter in the jungle garden behind their house, they'd been careful. Yet no menstrual cramps had appeared to put a damper on their lovemaking. It was entirely possible that the hormonal changes of impending motherhood accounted for the wired, anxious look he sometimes saw on her face.

Aaron decided to ask her what was going on. But he knew *now* wasn't the right time to do it. Troon's homecoming would mark their first attempt at entertaining as a couple and Kendra had gone all out to make it a success. A serious discussion at the last minute might throw her off balance. He'd wait until evening, after their guests had gone.

She burrowed deeper under the covers when he tried to wake her. "C'mon, sleepyhead," he persisted. "Up and at 'em. Rosa's got the coffee on—I can smell it. And from the sound of things, she and Clive are hard at work on the turkey."

Reluctantly Kendra's eyes opened. "What time is it?"

He grinned. "7:02 a.m. Since it's a holiday, I let you sleep late."

"You're all heart."

"Can I help it if I wanted your company?"

Waking up a little more, she heard the sounds of a children's show flowing from the portable TV set she'd bought for Rosa's use in the kitchen. Clive's excited chatter as he helped his mother stuff the twenty-six-pound bird that would be the centerpiece of their feast and Rosa's low-pitched replies formed a pleasant counterpoint.

By tonight I might find myself out on my ear, Kendra thought. But she couldn't allow herself more than a passing shudder. For the time being, all her energies had to be concentrated on making Troon's homecoming a happy one.

She was unusually quiet as she and Aaron tackled grapefruit, whole wheat toast and coffee at a kitchen table groaning with Rosa's luscious-looking pies and ready-to-bake casseroles. For some reason she kept thinking of

Arn Song. Maybe if I could finish forgiving Song for having the baby I wanted, she reasoned, I could forgive myself for not being able to give Aaron a child. Not to mention for making such a mess of things. That way, even if he ended up hating me, I wouldn't lose my self-respect.

They weren't scheduled to go over to the hospital for rounds until about 1:00 p.m. After breakfast Aaron went upstairs to hang some brightly colored posters and a bulletin board he'd picked up for Troon at a local frame shop. Next, though they had a regular lawn service, he went outdoors to do some pruning and mulching in the yard.

Mulling over her thoughts about Song, Kendra hung around inside, assisting Rosa with a variety of tasks and setting the table. When Aaron came downstairs shortly after noon, already showered and dressed to put in an appearance at the hospital, she was still in her jeans.

"Better get a move on if you're coming with me," he admonished, giving her derriere a friendly swat.

In the works all morning, an idea was finally taking shape. She hesitated. "Two of my patients checked out yesterday and you haven't added anyone to the list. That leaves the little Nelson girl. Do you suppose you could look in on her for me, just this once?"

Aaron had already made a similar concession to one of her fellow residents who wanted to spend the holiday with his grandparents in West Palm Beach. He could hardly refuse Kendra the same favor simply because she was his wife. He just wished he knew what was going on in her head.

"I'd be happy to," he said at last. "But what's the point? Rosa can manage without your help. And you'll be going to the hospital with me, anyway, to pick up Troon."

This time Kendra's silence was more pronounced. "Please don't think I wouldn't like to," she answered finally. "But there's something I have to do."

Though he waited, she didn't volunteer what that something was. Turning down Rosa's offer of a sandwich, he left for the hospital early. A few minutes later Kendra was showered and dressed.

"I have to go out for a while," she told the housekeeper, hurriedly snatching up her keys and purse. "Any last-minute items I can get you at the store?"

Rosa smiled and shook her head. "No, thanks, Dr. Dash. I've got everything under control. But don't stay away all afternoon. That turkey's starting to smell mighty good. And, if you ask me, the anticipation of eating it is half the fun."

Kendra paused to inhale the delicious aroma on her way out the door. "You're right...it smells scrumptious," she agreed. "I won't be long."

For once, as he began rounds at the hospital, Aaron found it difficult to concentrate. Kendra wasn't acting like herself and he was worried that things wouldn't go well that afternoon. I should have asked what was bothering her while I had the chance, he thought. Just then his page sounded and he phoned the operator. An emergency case had come in.

At that moment Kendra was in a south Tampa neighborhood, clutching the folded piece of paper on which she'd scribbled Arn Song's address. The corresponding apartment complex where she found herself was dreary and poorly maintained. She wondered if Song still lived there. Maybe with the income from Pran's trust she'd been able to move to a better place.

After a prolonged search, she found the correct building and apartment number. Walking up to the door, she pressed the buzzer. Following a brief delay, the slender, old-young woman she remembered from the Star of Siam grocery appeared.

"Mrs. Jenkin!" Song exclaimed.

Bowing several times, the Cambodian woman invited her inside. To Kendra's distinct discomfort, Song began to shower her with gratitude for Pran's trust. "You so generous!" Song exclaimed. "Because of what you do, Pran's future secure."

Kendra shook her head. "You mustn't thank me," she replied. "Pran has a right to support from his father's estate. I'm only sorry I couldn't find you earlier."

Clearly self-conscious over her position vis-à-vis Glenn Jenkins's widow, Song couldn't seem to think of anything else to say. The two women stood there looking at each other. What a fragile, unfortunate person Song is, Kendra thought. It's not her fault I had that stupid accident when I was a teen. *Not her fault I can't have a baby.*

The last trace of resentment left her heart. "By the way, my name isn't Mrs. Jenkins anymore," she said. "It's Dr. Dash. After Glenn's death I went back to school and earned a medical degree. A few weeks ago I remarried. My husband and I are about to adopt a Cambodian refugee child."

Song's eyes widened at the news. "Is this true?" she asked in astonishment. "You very loving person, I think. Have good heart."

Kendra ducked her head at the compliment. Yet in a way she knew it was apt. Love had drawn her into the quagmire she faced. And, though she had no legitimate excuse for deceiving Aaron, she thought suddenly that, if he could meet Song and Pran, he might understand how much her childlessness had hurt her. Maybe he'd focus on their love and not what she couldn't give him. Forgive her foolishness in not telling him the truth.

Watching her with a concerned expression, Song offered to share the tea, rice and cooked vegetables that would be the Arns' evening meal.

"I'm sorry, I can't stay," Kendra said, shaking off her private musings with a smile. "It's Thanksgiving and we're expecting company. Have you and Pran invited anyone?"

Song shook her head. "Not have relatives here."

It seemed a situation made to order. Like her, Song needed to forgive herself. And the turkey Rosa was basting was more than ample for another two people.

Her voice was firm. "Then you're coming home with me. I'll be happy to drive you back after dinner."

The Cambodian woman shrank into herself at the very idea. "No, please," she whispered. "Not right we impose."

With the issuance of her invitation, Kendra's usual gung-ho energy had reasserted itself. She wasn't about to take no for an answer.

"You must," she insisted. "It's time you and Pran learned to honor a venerable American tradition. And there'll be other Cambodians present—the couple who rescued our son, Troon, from a refugee camp. You'll feel right at home."

Kendra wanted to cheer when they made it back to the house before Aaron and Troon arrived. Asking Rosa to set two extra places and settling Pran with Clive and a stack of Christmas catalogs in front of the television set, she turned to Song. "Would you do me a favor?" she asked.

"Of course," Song answered. "What you want me to do?"

They managed to scrounge up some shelf paper left over from Rosa's reorganization of the kitchen. Working together, they constructed a huge banner that read Welcome Home, Troon in both English and Khmer. With a hammer, tacks and Song's help steadying the stepladder, Kendra affixed it over the archway to the dining room.

Climbing down, she stood back to survey their handiwork. "Doesn't it look great?" she exclaimed as she and Song smiled at each other. "I only wish we had some balloons!"

Full of adrenaline and released vigor, she turned next to the phone. One by one she dialed their guests and asked that they come over as soon as possible. "I should have thought of it before," she told each of them. "But I'd like you to be on hand to welcome Troon when he arrives."

Houm and Ny drove up in a taxi Kendra had dispatched for them. "Your house beautiful," Ny commented via her husband, stopping to pet Tofu who was skittering about underfoot.

The living room—cozy now with a fire on the hearth, comfortable overstuffed sofas and chairs and the Persian rug Kendra had once imagined there—was buzzing with people by the time Aaron and Troon walked in the door. For a split second a hush fell over the room. Then, per Kendra's instructions, a shout went up in two languages.

"Welcome home!"

Seconds later she was holding out her arms. And Aaron was going into them, drawing Troon into the circle of their embrace. Spontaneously the group around them started applauding. There were some very misty eyes.

"Who are the Oriental woman and little Amerasian boy?" Aaron whispered to Kendra a few minutes later as he fixed a round of drinks. "I don't remember meeting them before."

"Arn Song was Glenn's mistress," Kendra answered. "The boy is his child."

He'd heard about Pran's trust, of course. But he hadn't remembered the Arns' names, or realized that anything remotely approaching a friendship had been struck. "I suppose *they're* the reason you couldn't come to the hospital this afternoon," he said.

"Umm-hmm." Though she still dreaded confessing her secret, Kendra couldn't help but feel rather pleased with herself.

Aaron was obviously pleased with her, as well. "You never cease to amaze me, Redhead," he remarked, giving her fanny a pat. "We'll talk about this later. I want to hear the whole story straight from your pretty mouth."

Cooked and served to twelve people by the incomparable Rosa, dinner was nothing short of magnificent. Aaron beamed at Kendra across a candlelit table surrounded by faces of various colors. A happy, multilingual babble of voices filled the room.

At first Troon had been too overwhelmed to speak. Gradually his reserve melted, no doubt aided and abetted by Tofu's presence under the table where the rambunctious kitten was begging for scraps. He also seemed comforted by the hum of chatter in the Cambodian tongue. Abruptly, weeks of patience on Kendra's part were rewarded when he felt secure enough to try out a few words of English on Clive. Her heart turned over as Troon glanced at her out of the corner of his eye with a shy but proud expression.

Finally even the pies had been demolished to the last crumb. A feeling of well-being pervaded the room. As she looked around, Kendra realized her notion of what *family* meant had expanded a hundredfold. A woman didn't have to carry an infant inside her body for nine months to give her husband a child. Though she and Aaron had been married only a short time, she'd already done that for him.

Similarly, she didn't need a dozen brothers and sisters, aunts, uncles and cousins to hold a family feast. In addition to our son, everyone in this room is part of our true family, she thought, exchanging a loving look with her husband. It's possible you'll be very angry with me when I tell you what I have to tell you. I can only pray you'll forgive me. I'm going to do my absolute best to make you understand.

At last it was time for the landmark evening to end. Hugging the Johanssens as they were about to depart, Kendra impulsively extended an invitation to everyone present. "Same time, same place, *next* year," she said. "Okay?"

The offer was readily accepted and she tossed Aaron a challenging look. Try to get out of *that,* she dared him silently, pushing down the anxiety that threatened to surface again.

Puzzled by the glance, Aaron raised one brow. All evening Kendra had been like a candle burning at both ends. They really did have to talk.

Her back to him now, she was saying good-night to Bess.

"Looks like I can stop worrying about one of my favorite people," the nursing director was saying. "From what I can tell, you've got more happiness than one person can handle, my dear."

Oh, I can handle it, Kendra answered silently, hugging Bess in turn. Holding on to it might be the trick. Yet, uneasy though she was, her heart was filled with hope.

After their friends from the hospital had gone, she and Aaron drove the Arns and the Morngs home to their respective apartments while Rosa put Troon and Clive to bed. For that night at least, they decided, Clive would occupy the second twin bed in Troon's room.

When they returned, Rosa had the dishwasher humming and the place tidy. "If that rascal of mine gets noisy in the morning, you send him right down to me," she instructed with a broad smile.

By unspoken consent, Aaron and Kendra headed upstairs. Their ten-year-old, soon-to-be-adopted son was sleeping like a baby with his animal puppets arranged prominently on a shelf and the turkey's coveted wishbone tied to his bedpost with a red ribbon. Tofu was curled up in a furry ball by his feet. In the next bed, Clive lay sprawled on his stomach, his wiry brown body storing up energy for a day of exuberant play with his new friend.

Eleven o'clock, Kendra thought. And in the Dash household, all is *almost* well.

"It's been quite a day, hasn't it?" Aaron asked as they retired to the privacy of their bedroom. "Even though I have the strong feeling I've been missing something."

Here goes, thought Kendra, a distinct lump in her throat. The inevitable moment has arrived. If I lose him, I don't know how I'm going to live with it. To her, as he removed his tweed jacket and cranberry-colored tie while waiting for her to speak, he was the most special man in all the world.

"The reason I once told you we couldn't see each other after my residency was finished... and the reason I was afraid to let our marriage become a permanent one," she confessed in a little rush, "is that I can't have a baby. Not ever. One morning when I was fifteen years old, I climbed up on the roof of my father's barn trying to rescue a kitten that looked remarkably like Tofu. My foot slipped on a loose single and I fell. There was a great deal of internal bleeding. I ruptured my spleen and..."

The velvet pools in Aaron's gold-flecked eyes widened. He'd noticed the faded scar on her stomach. But he hadn't envisioned anything like what she was describing. "Your uterus was irreparably damaged and they had to do a hysterectomy," he said slowly.

She nodded. "They managed to save one ovary so I wouldn't have to take hormones."

"And you thought I'd reject you simply because you can't have a baby?"

Tears stung her eyelids. "What was I supposed to think? You kept saying how much you wanted to father a child someday!"

A frown drew his dark brows together. "When did I say that?"

"Don't you remember?" Her tone was anguished. "The first time was the afternoon I brought you home from the airport. You were telling me about wanting to adopt Lin and Troon. 'Like most men,' you said, 'I'd like to father a child.' And then, the first night we slept together after we were married..."

By now the remark to which she alluded was ringing in Aaron's ears. *I rather like the idea of giving you a baby,* he'd said. No wonder she'd turned away from him.

Yet how could he have known? She hadn't given him a clue, probably because of his earlier comment. Yet he'd only made that one to reassure her he wasn't a dead-end street if she was counting on biological motherhood. The revelation about her teenage accident explained a lot of things.

"You can't begin to guess how much I'd like to give you a child," she whispered. "I know I should have told you. If you don't want us to stay married now, I'll understand."

"Kendra, you little fool!"

With a growl that was part exasperation, part overwhelming affection, he pulled her into his arms. He could feel her trembling. For a moment he simply held her close.

Then, "I admit that, if you were able to conceive for us someday, I'd like nothing better," he said, determined every card they possessed should end up on the table. "But compared to a life without you, that loss is insignificant. We can always have more children. A few years down the road, when Troon can't remember what it was like not to be our son and you're ready from a career standpoint, we can adopt a little girl. God knows, there are plenty of children who need us. . . ."

He was saying it didn't matter—that he wanted their marriage to last!

"Oh, Aaron..." she cried. "I love you so!" Tears of joy replacing those of apprehension and shame at the way she'd kept an important truth from him, she kissed him lovingly on the mouth. "Can you ever forgive me for not telling you about this sooner?"

"Sweetheart, there's nothing to forgive. I can imagine how you felt. I only hope that, in the future—"

Briefly she shut her eyes. "I promise," she said. "No more secrets. I've been so miserable, worrying about what would happen to Troon if we split up over this. Worrying about *you*. . ."

He shook his head. "I was going to say that from now on I'll pay better attention to what's going on with you. As for splitting up. . . don't you know I'd never allow that to happen? Not in a million years!"

At this moment, Kendra thought, I must be the happiest woman on the face of the earth. Her marriage secure and her heart light for the first time in months, she reached for his shirt buttons. "I do now," she answered. "Don't you think it's time we went to bed?"

Spilling over with relief, gratitude and love for each other, they moved to set a passionate seal on the day's events. Disrobed with exquisite care by her handsome, dark-haired husband, Kendra took off his things in turn. She couldn't get enough of touching him. Moments later they were turning back the top sheet on their bed. There won't be any more holding back between us, she thought as she came into his arms.

Sensation took over as he kissed her breasts and trailed one hand lower to the nub of her womanhood. Though her craving for him was boundless, she didn't want him to hurry. She was quivering at the brink, ready to go off like a Fourth-of-July rocket, when at last he entered. Deep and implosive, his thrusts relentlessly expanded her reservoir of heat.

When it arose, the peak of their communion was like nothing she'd ever experienced, though its force recalled the way he'd taken her on the rain-soaked grass. Dissolving in a paroxysm of shudders, she was only half aware of the stifled moans that escaped her. Above hers, Aaron's face was a mask of rapture and delight.

Drifting down like a half-extinguished ember, Kendra nestled in his arms. Minutes passed before she was ready to explain the role her coming to terms with Song had played in helping her set things straight between them.

Keenly attuned now to her every mood and feeling, Aaron understood. "Guess what Ny said to me this evening," he teased gently.

Her murmur was filled with contentment. "I have no idea."

"That it looked like I'd finally caught my pig on ice. Of course, I doubt she has more than a theoretical concept of what ice *is*, other than cubes from the refrigerator...."

"You idiot!" Rousing herself, Kendra tickled him mercilessly in the ribs. "If Ny doesn't fully comprehend your offbeat figures of speech, it's nobody's fault but yours!"

Though she hadn't demanded to know his answer, he decided to tell her, anyway. "I replied that I'd caught the woman and child I wanted, and that I couldn't imagine a greater happiness," he said, imprisoning her errant hands in his. "Don't be surprised if, when we're making patient rounds in the morning, my running shoes are several feet off the ground."

* * * * *

FASHION A WHOLE NEW YOU

WIN

CARS, TRIPS, CASH!

SILHOUETTE® OFFICIAL SWEEPSTAKES RULES

NO PURCHASE NECESSARY

1. To enter, complete an Official Entry Form or 3"× 5" index card by hand-printing, in plain block letters, your complete name, address, phone number and age, and mailing it to: Silhouette Fashion A Whole New You Sweepstakes, P.O. Box 9056, Buffalo, NY 14269-9056.

   No responsibility is assumed for lost, late or misdirected mail. Entries must be sent separately with first class postage affixed, and be received no later than December 31, 1991 for eligibility.

2. Winners will be selected by D.L. Blair, Inc., an independent judging organization whose decisions are final, in random drawings to be held on January 30, 1992 in Blair, NE at 10:00 a.m. from among all eligible entries received.

3. The prizes to be awarded and their approximate retail values are as follows: Grand Prize — A brand-new Ford Explorer 4×4 plus a trip for two (2) to Hawaii, including round-trip air transportation, six (6) nights hotel accommodation, a $1,400 meal/spending money stipend and $2,000 cash toward a new fashion wardrobe (approximate value: $28,000) or $15,000 cash; two (2) Second Prizes — A trip to Hawaii, including round-trip air transportation, six (6) nights hotel accommodation, a $1,400 meal/spending money stipend and $2,000 cash toward a new fashion wardrobe (approximate value: $11,000) or $5,000 cash; three (3) Third Prizes — $2,000 cash toward a new fashion wardrobe. All prizes are valued in U.S. currency. Travel award air transportation is from the commercial airport nearest winner's home. Travel is subject to space and accommodation availability, and must be completed by June 30, 1993. Sweepstakes offer is open to residents of the U.S. and Canada who are 21 years of age or older as of December 31, 1991, except residents of Puerto Rico, employees and immediate family members of Torstar Corp., its affiliates, subsidiaries, and all agencies, entities and persons connected with the use, marketing, or conduct of this sweepstakes. All federal, state, provincial, municipal and local laws apply. Offer void wherever prohibited by law. Taxes and/or duties, applicable registration and licensing fees, are the sole responsibility of the winners. Any litigation within the province of Quebec respecting the conduct and awarding of a prize may be submitted to the Régie des loteries et courses du Québec. All prizes will be awarded; winners will be notified by mail. No substitution of prizes is permitted.

4. Potential winners must sign and return any required Affidavit of Eligibility/Release of Liability within 30 days of notification. In the event of noncompliance within this time period, the prize may be awarded to an alternate winner. Any prize or prize notification returned as undeliverable may result in the awarding of that prize to an alternate winner. By acceptance of their prize, winners consent to use of their names, photographs or their likenesses for purposes of advertising, trade and promotion on behalf of Torstar Corp. without further compensation. Canadian winners must correctly answer a time-limited arithmetical question in order to be awarded a prize.

5. For a list of winners (available after 3/31/92), send a separate stamped, self-addressed envelope to: Silhouette Fashion A Whole New You Sweepstakes, P.O. Box 4665, Blair, NE 68009.

PREMIUM OFFER TERMS

To receive your gift, complete the Offer Certificate according to directions. Be certain to enclose the required number of "Fashion A Whole New You" proofs of product purchase (which are found on the last page of every specially marked "Fashion A Whole New You" Silhouette or Harlequin romance novel). Requests must be received no later than December 31, 1991. Limit: four (4) gifts per name, family, group, organization or address. Items depicted are for illustrative purposes only and may not be exactly as shown. Please allow 6 to 8 weeks for receipt of order. Offer good while quantities of gifts last. In the event an ordered gift is no longer available, you will receive a free, previously unpublished Silhouette or Harlequin book for every proof of purchase you have submitted with your request, plus a refund of the postage and handling charge you have included. Offer good in the U.S. and Canada only.

SLFW-SWPR

See previous page for details.